PAINTED

PERFECTLY IMPERFECT SERIES

scars

NEVA ALTAJ

AUTHOR'S NOTE

Dear reader, there are a few Russian words mentioned in the book, so here are the translations and clarifications:

Pakhan – пахан is the head of Russian mafia.

Bratva – братва́ is Russian organized crime or Russian mafia.

Malysh – малыш (little one) is used as an endearment in lieu of "baby". The word is masculine but can be used as gender neutral. There's also a feminine version – малышка (*malyshka*), and that, too, can be used to address a (female) partner, but most prefer "malysh".

Kukolka – куколка (little doll) is a diminutive of "*kukla*" which means "doll".

Milaya – милая (dear, loved one) is used as an endearment in lieu of "darling or honey".

Piroshki – пирожки́ (hand pies) are small pastries filled with finely chopped meat, vegetables or fruit and can be baked or fried.

Morozhenoe – мороженое (ice cream).

A note regarding Russian surnames: Most married Russian women's last names are formed by adding an "a" at the end of their husband's surname (e.g. Petrov, Petrova). Russians living abroad may adjust to local rules and both husband and wife will have the same ending on their driver's license and other documents to avoid confusion (Roman Petrov and Nina Petrov). However, the wife would be still addressed as Nina Petrova by Russians, no matter what country they lived in.

PAINTED

scars

Roman

BEEP. *BEEP.*

Strong hospital smell. Looks like I lived.

I try opening my eyes. It doesn't work. The anesthesia is probably just starting to wear off. At least there is no more pain. There are hushed voices coming from my left, but they are subdued, and even though they sound familiar, I can't recognize them.

Beep. Beep.

"Can he hear us?"

"No. He's heavily sedated."

Beep.

"Will he live?"

"Yes. Unfortunately. The wounds on his chest were not that bad. They patched him up."

"We can always try again. Pin it on the Italians again."

"Too risky. People are loyal to the pakhan. Anyone suspects me, and I'll end up in a ditch."

Beep.

"Well, there might be a silver lining. The shrapnel shattered his knee."

"So?"

"Doctor said he won't walk again. If someone more capable comes into the picture . . . people, no matter how loyal, will hardly stand behind a pakhan who's in a wheelchair when presented with a better option."

"Well, I guess we did well after all."

There are two sets of steps leaving, and then a door closes.

CHAPTER

one

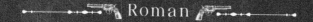 Roman

Three months later

THERE ARE NEVER ENOUGH DRUGS.

I put the sheet filled with notes on the pile of papers on my desk and focus on the numbers on the laptop screen.

"Call Sergei." I lean back in my wheelchair and look at Maxim, who is sitting on the other side of my desk. "I need him to arrange two additional shipments this month."

"He already negotiated the quantities with Mendoza for the quarter. I'm not sure the Mexicans can double it on such short notice."

"They will. Now, tell me what the fuck happened because I know that look well, and I know I won't like the answer."

"Samuel Grey embezzled three million dollars. Our money."

I sigh and shake my head. "Who is Samuel Grey, why

did he have access to our money, and how did he manage to do that?"

"Our real estate mediator. The money was meant for buying two more lots near the north warehouse. Grey thought he could borrow our money for a week for some investment which ended up being a Ponzi scheme."

How much of an idiot would a person have to be to steal from the Bratva? Sometimes I'm amazed by people's stupidity.

"Can he pay it back?" I ask.

"No."

"Kill him. And make an example out of him."

"I had something else in mind. People . . . people are starting to talk, Roman. We need a distraction, fast. I think Grey can provide that distraction."

"Oh? And what have they been talking about?" I've known Maxim since he started working for my father two decades ago as a foot soldier. The old pakhan never could determine a person's potential. Wasting a man as capable as Maxim by assigning him to basic fieldwork was one of many mistakes I corrected the moment I became the pakhan twelve years ago. Right after I killed the bastard.

"You. Still being unmarried."

That's old news. "But that's not all, is it? What else?" I narrow my eyes at Maxim.

He's not looking at me, his gaze focused on something on the wall behind me. "There are rumors that you won't be able to run the Bratva much longer and someone else will take your place. Someone more . . . physically able."

"And do you share their opinion?"

"Do not insult me, Roman. You know I've always stood by you, and I'll keep doing so. Even if I don't think you're the most capable pakhan the Bratva ever had. But you've been holed up here for three months. You haven't been to any of our clubs to check on the operations like you did at least once a month before the explosion. And you haven't been seen with a woman."

"So, the status of my sex life is a better indicator of my ability to run the Bratva than the fact we doubled our profit the last two months?"

"People need the feel of stability, Roman. They still remember how your father took over the previous pakhan's place and the chaos that followed. The Bratva lost more than fifty people to internal skirmishes, and the business was devastated. They need to know that it won't happen again. A wife means there will be an heir who'll be ready to take over your place when the time comes, without internal war or people dying."

"I won't tie myself to some random woman for life just to pacify our ranks."

"Let me show you something." Maxim takes out his phone and starts scrolling. "My daughter went to school with Samuel's daughter. They weren't close friends or anything, but they hung out together often, and I remember her showing me the videos she took. I asked her to send me one of those last night when I heard what Samuel Grey did."

"What would videos of teenagers have to do with my ability to lead the Bratva?"

"Well, she's not a teenager anymore. Nina Grey finished art studies at The Art Institute here in Chicago in two years instead of four, and she's currently the most sought-after young artist in the country. Her paintings sell for four figures each."

"So what, we'll hire her to paint us a family portrait?"

I pinch the bridge of my nose. "You're barely fifty. Are you going senile prematurely?"

"We aren't hiring her to paint us a portrait. We'll be blackmailing her. Her father's life for her services."

"To do what?"

"To marry you, Roman. Well, temporarily at least."

I stare at my second-in-command for a few seconds and then burst out laughing. "You are out of your mind."

"Am I?" He crosses his hands and leans back. "And what does the therapist say? About your leg."

"He expects me to be able to regain up to 80 percent of its use."

"What does that mean?"

"It means crutches in the worst-case scenario. A cane in the best."

"That's good. How much time are we talking about? A month?"

I look him right in the eyes and grind my teeth. "At least six more months of physical therapy."

"Shit, Roman." He reaches with his hand and squeezes his temples. "We can't wait that long. We need something now, or we'll have riots."

I look out the window and sigh. Maxim is usually always right. "You're saying it's either me having two functioning legs or a wife? I won't be walking any time soon, Maxim."

"Well, in that case, we're getting you a wife until you do."

"That's ridiculous. I can't blackmail a woman I don't know into pretending to be my wife for six months, especially one who has no connection to our world. She'll probably be terrified. No one will buy that."

"Watch this," Maxim says and thrusts his phone into my hand.

The video is grainy, probably because it was taken years ago, but the lighting is good and I can see the inside of a room with several teenagers sitting in a semicircle, their backs to the camera. The only person whose face is visible is a dark-haired girl sitting cross-legged before the audience. The camera zooms in, bringing her pixie like features and dark eyes into focus. I wonder what she looks like now.

"Can you do Mrs. Nolan?" someone from the semicircle asks. "When she talks about her cats?"

"Again?" The young Nina Grey groans. "How about someone new? Maybe a politician?"

There is a collective sound of displeasure and several teens shout, "Mrs. Nolan!" The young Nina shakes her head then smiles and closes her eyes. When she opens them a few seconds later and starts talking, I find myself pulling the phone closer, completely in awe.

She's speaking, but I don't pay attention to the actual words. I'm completely absorbed in watching the mimicry on her face, the way her right eye trembles slightly when she speaks, how she accentuates the words. All of a sudden, it's like she's a completely different person.

"How old is she in this video?" I ask without removing my eyes from the screen.

"Fourteen. Amazing, isn't she?"

In the video, someone shouts another name and points to a girl sitting at the end of the semicircle. Nina Grey laughs, closes her eyes in concentration, and then starts a new act. Again, she takes on a completely new persona with her posture, and the way her hands move while she talks. The girl on the side watches her, then laughs and covers her face with her hand. Nina replicates the motion to the detail, even the way the girl's shoulders rise a little while she laughs. I don't think I ever witnessed something like that.

I look up to find Maxim smiling in satisfaction. "As you can see, there shouldn't be any problems with her pretending to be anything you need her to be."

"You're serious about this?" I still find this idea of his completely idiotic.

"Desperate times require desperate measures, Roman. We need to shut down the rumors, and we need to do it now."

"In that case, the wife it is." I slam the laptop closed. "Shit!"

Nina

I put my bag on the recliner and turn around in the living room. It's been months since I've been here, but it looks like nothing has changed. The same white curtains and carpet, white and beige furniture, empty white walls. So much white—it looks sterile. I've always despised it. No wonder the first significant amount of money I earned, I used it to rent an apartment and get away from this bleakness.

"I'm home!" I shout.

A few seconds later there is a sound of clicking heels coming my way. My mom exits the kitchen and rushes toward me, her hands on her hips. Zara Grey is the complete opposite of me—tall and blonde, with full makeup on, and in a perfectly pressed dress. A white silky one. I want to groan.

"You are three hours late, I told you—" she stops mid-sentence. "Dear God, what have you done with yourself?"

"Can you be more specific?"

"The metal thing on your nose."

"It is called a piercing, Mom."

"People get diseases through those, Nina. When your father sees you, he'll have a heart attack."

"I'm twenty-four. I can do whatever I please with my body. And I've had it for years, I just remove it when I come here to avoid you pestering me. I forgot today."

"And why are you wearing all black? Did someone die?"

A few of my brain cells, for sure.

"I'm in a dark phase this month." I shrug.

My mom loves the clichés. I think they make her feel more comfortable, especially around me. She still finds my choice of a career hard to process. Maybe it would be easier for her if I drew flower arrangements or baby deer. I wonder what she'd have to say about my latest piece. It's still a work in progress, but there are no flowers or deer planned.

"Why do you have to be so strange all the time?"

"Works great with guys." I grin. "Men love strange women."

"I'm not so sure about that, honey."

God, she can't even get my sarcasm.

"When Dad called, he said it was urgent. Where is he?"

"In the study. He's been acting out of character the last few days. I think it has something to do with work, but he won't tell me anything. It seems . . . like he's scared of something."

My father is in a real estate business. Not many things to be scared of. I enter the hallway on the left and knock on the door of my father's study, without having the faintest idea how drastically my life is going to change when I get inside.

Half an hour later, I'm sitting in a recliner occupying the corner of the office and staring at my father, open-mouthed. "Is this a joke?"

"It's not a joke." He slumps his shoulders and passes a hand through his graying hair.

"Okay, let me get this straight. You stole money from the Russians and lost it, so now you're asking me to marry a Russian mob boss."

"I didn't steal anything, Nina." He throws his arms in the air, stands up, and starts pacing behind his desk. "I just borrowed it for a few days because I needed the funds for this deal. I never thought the guy was a fraud or that he'd take the money and vanish."

"You took the money, and you can't pay them back. How the fuck did you get involved with Russian mafia? What the hell were you thinking, Dad?"

"Don't talk to me like that!" He points an accusatory finger at me. "I'm your father!"

"You are asking me to marry a criminal to save your butt, for God's sake. I think I can talk to you any way I want, all things considered."

"Nina . . ."

"They expect me to marry their boss? Like, for real?"

"It's just temporary." He waves his hand in the air like it's not a big deal.

"But, why? Isn't there a line of mafia daughters somewhere wanting to marry the guy? It would be a dream come true for any of them, right? Why me?"

"They didn't say. These people don't explain themselves. They tell you what to do, and if you don't do it, you're dead."

"You really think they'll kill you?"

"Yes. I'm surprised they haven't already." He pauses his pacing and turns to face me. "If you don't do what they ask, I'm dead."

I take a deep breath and bury my hands in my hair, squeezing my head like it's going to help find a solution to this fuckup. Because I am not marrying anyone, fake marriage or not. "Okay, let's think. There must be some way to fix this. I have some savings, maybe fifty grand. I have my next exhibition in a month, and I should be able to get another twenty if I can manage to finish all fifteen pieces and they all sell. How much money can you get for the house?"

"Maybe eighty grand. Or ninety, if we sell the furniture as well. I can get ten more for the car."

"Good. That places us at somewhere around one hundred and seventy thousand. Will that be enough? How much do you owe them?"

"Three million."

I must have had a minor stroke because there is no way he said the words I just heard him say. "Can you please repeat that?"

"I owe them three million dollars."

I stare at him with my mouth wide open. "Dear God, Dad!"

I bend down and place my forehead on my knees, trying to control my breathing. I'm not marriage material—no one in their right mind would offer three million dollars in exchange for six months of marriage. There must be a catch.

"He's ninety, isn't he?" I mumble into my knees.

"I don't know how old their pakhan is, but I don't think he's ninety."

"Eighty then. I'm so relieved." I'm going to be sick.

"They said it'll be a marriage in name only. You won't have to . . . you know."

"Sleep with him? Well, if he's eighty, then he probably can't have sex. That's good. Eighty is good."

"Nina, I-I am so sorry. If you don't want to go through with this, that's okay. I'll figure something out."

I straighten up and look at my father who's now sitting slumped in his chair, his hair in disarray and his eyes blood-shot. He looks so old and frail all of a sudden.

"Unless you plan to go to the police, there's nothing else to be done, is there?" I ask.

"You know I can't go tattle on the Russian mafia to the police. They would kill us all."

Of course, they'd kill us. I close my eyes and sigh. "Okay. I'll do it."

My father watches me for a few seconds, then places his hands over his face and starts crying. I want to cry as well, but there's no point.

"I suppose they'll set up a meeting, or something, where we'll discuss the details."

"They already did. We are meeting the pakhan in an hour."

I look at my father and bury my hands in my hair. "Perfect. I'm just going to the bathroom to puke up my lunch, and I'll meet you at the front door in five."

CHAPTER
Two

 Roman

A GIRL BRINGS MY DRINK, PLACES IT ON THE TABLE in front of me, and without looking up, turns and runs back toward the kitchen. I look around, noting the drab tablecloths and mismatching chairs. The place is a dump. It closed last month, which is exactly why I picked it for this meeting. A sound of a phone ringing pierces the silence.

"They're here," Maxim says from his spot behind me. "She came with her father."

"Let the girl in. The father is to stay outside."

I take a sip of whiskey and focus my eyes on the glass door on the other side of the room. There's a knock and my man standing by the door opens it, letting the girl inside.

For some reason, I expected her to be taller. She is a tiny thing, not much over five feet. Her long midnight-black hair is in two thick braids on either side of her face, and if you overlook her breasts, she could pass as a teenager. She's even dressed like one—torn black jeans, a black hoodie, and those black boots I've seen emo kids wearing.

I close my eyes for a second and shake my head. This will never work. I'm planning to tell Maxim to send her away when her head turns toward me, and the words die on my lips. She has the same features I saw on the video, but her face has lost its childlike appearance with round cheeks. Instead of a cute teenage girl, an unbelievably beautiful woman stands there, watching me with something that looks very much like anger. Her eyes connect with mine and one perfect black eyebrow arches in question.

"Miss Grey," I say and motion toward the empty chair on the other side of the table "Please, join us."

I wait for her to cower, maybe flinch, but she doesn't seem even a little bit disturbed by the situation. She approaches, keeping her gaze connected with mine all the while. She doesn't take the chair as instructed but stands right in front of me and looks me over. I focus on her face, waiting to see her reaction when she notices the wheelchair. There isn't any.

"You are not what I expected, Mr. Petrov," she says, and I have to give it to her—the girl has balls.

"How so, Miss Grey?"

"I expected you to be eighty." She purses her lips.

Is she actually that composed and unperturbed, or is this another of her acts, I wonder? If it's an act, she's really good.

"I'm thirty-five." I take a sip from my glass. "Now that we cleared that up, let's talk business. Your father explained what's expected of you?"

"He did. And I have some questions." She takes the end of one of her braids and starts winding it around her finger. Not so relaxed as she's trying to present herself, after all. "And since we will be calling this a business transaction, I have one condition."

14

"A condition? You are in no position to negotiate the terms, Miss Grey, but let's hear it."

"You'll let my father go. This . . . transaction will stay between the two of us. He's out of the picture."

"I'll think about it. Now, let's hear the questions."

"Why do you need a fake wife?"

"None of your concern. And the marriage won't be fake. Next question."

She narrows her eyes at me. "What happens after six months?"

"You'll get the divorce papers and be on your merry way."

"How will we go about the wedding thing? Just go and sign the papers?"

I lean back in my chair and regard her. "We need to make some things clear, Miss Grey. I don't need a wife just on paper. If anyone suspects we're not crazy in love, and this marriage is a sham, your father is dead. And you'll be joining him."

She blinks and looks at me with confusion clearly shown on her face. "You expect us to live together for six months?"

"Of course. How else would people believe the marriage?"

It looks like something finally manages to rattle her, because she just stands there staring at me with wide eyes, saying nothing. I have a feeling there are not many things that can leave Nina Grey speechless.

"There'll be a party on Saturday," I continue. "You'll attend with your father. We'll meet and become besotted with each other. I'll take you home with me that evening, and we won't leave my room for two days."

"Am I expected to have sex with you?"

She says it in an even voice as if asking about the weather, but I see it in her eyes—a restrained terror. I'm pretty sure no one else would notice it because she looks so perfectly composed on the outside. But inflicting fear in people is something I do on regular basis, and I see it as clear as day. She's horrified.

"No," I say, then decide to try rattling her a little. "Unless you want to, of course."

"Thank you for the offer, Mr. Petrov, but I will have to decline." She lets go of her braid and puts her hands in the back pockets of her jeans.

Even though I expected her to say no, for some reason, her reply stings.

"And what will we be doing for two days in your room, Mr. Petrov?"

"As far as anyone else is concerned, we will be having lots and lots of sex. In reality, you can do whatever you please." I motion with my hand through the air. "Watch Netflix. Solve crosswords. I don't care. I'll be working the whole time anyway."

"Lovely. And what happens after those two days of marathon sex?"

"I lose my mind over you. We marry in a few weeks. After that, you'll play your role of a crazy-in-love wife." I shrug. "What you do with your free time is up to you, as long as you play your part along the way."

"And? That's it?"

"That's it."

"Do you truly think that someone will believe in this . . . charade?"

"Well, that's up to you, Miss Grey. Your father's life is at stake."

"And you? Can you pull off your part?"

"Which part?"

"That of a man who is mindlessly infatuated with his wife. You don't seem like that kind."

"I guess you'll have to wait and see for yourself," I say and smile. "Do we have a deal, Miss Grey?"

I can almost see the wheels turning in her head—weighing the options, pros and cons—looking for an out. But there isn't one and we both know it. I catch the exact moment she accepts the situation—just a slight hardening around her jaw as she grinds her teeth.

"We have a deal, Mr. Petrov."

Nina

The evening is unusually warm, but I still feel cold all over as I step out of the restaurant. My father grabs my arm and hastily ushers me toward the car, asking me questions along the way, but I can't focus on his words. I open the passenger door and sit down. My legs are trembling. Looks like the adrenaline ran out and I'm feeling the aftereffects.

I've never been as scared as the moment I entered that restaurant, wondering if they had changed their minds and decided to kill us. Staying composed and cool in front of that shark of a man required tremendous self-control. I almost slipped a few times. But, if he thought, even for a moment, that I couldn't play his game, my father and I were as good as dead. The wheelchair didn't fool me, I knew who I was facing the moment our gazes met—a stone-cold killer.

Roman Petrov. I assumed he was some elderly guy with a beer belly and receding hairline. Why would he be blackmailing a woman into marriage otherwise? I couldn't have been more wrong.

During our conversation, I tried my best to keep my eyes fixated on his, but I still managed to steal a few glances elsewhere. The man is incredibly handsome. That was evident even in the scarce light. I couldn't pinpoint his height, with him in a sitting position and me standing, but our heads were at the same level. He surely had more than a foot on me. It's not a nice thing to say, but I was relieved he was in a wheelchair. Being near tall men is a serious problem for me, and the idea of being stuck together with one for six months sent me into a shitstorm of panic.

"Nina!" my father yells. "Are you even hearing me? What the hell happened inside? I tried to go in but the goons wouldn't let me."

I take a deep breath and, watching the cars pass us on the driveway, start giving him the short version of the deal I made with the head of the Russian underworld. I share only the basics of the marriage agreement. The less he knows, the better.

"No word about any of this to Mom," I say when we arrive in front of the house, "and make sure you act as if you never met Petrov on Saturday. He said if anything goes wrong, the deal is off."

"What do you mean?"

"It means that if anyone, Mom included, suspects I'm not crazy in love with that son of a bitch, we're dead."

CHAPTER Three

 Nina

I LOOK AT THE PILE OF DRESSES I'VE JUST FINISHED trying on and feel the crazy need to sit on the small stool in the changing room and cry. All of them are designed for women taller than me and blessed with huge breasts. Every dress so far has made me look comical, like a girl who's been playing in her mother's closet.

I've been thinking about the party this whole week, absorbed in different scenarios that might happen after I arrive. It's occupied my every waking thought, and I' completely forgot to buy a dress. The realization came only this morning while I was eating my cereal, and I almost fainted. I always have problems finding dresses that fit, so finding one in a few hours would be an impossible feat.

Fast-forward, and here I am—entering the fifth hour of my fruitless shopping spree, and I still haven't found anything remotely suitable for a fancy event. I love wearing elegant clothes, but I used to get so frustrated each time I tried to buy something, I stopped looking and focused on my casual wardrobe. I would never tell anyone, but most of the time I shop in teen sections. Based on the tags, I am fourteen years old. And tonight, I would rather go in my jeans than in a dress from the teen prom rack.

My phone rings, and I fish it out from my jeans pocket on the chair and look at the unknown caller on the screen. Probably a wrong number. I put the phone back on top of my folded jeans, letting it ring, and reach for the last of the dresses to try out. It's a beautiful silky green thing, and it would look amazing . . . on someone else. Just looking at it is enough to see that the waistline would fall below my waist, almost at my hips. The phone rings again, and it's the same number. I reject the call just to have them call once more a minute later. Well, isn't someone persistent? They'll probably just keep calling, so better to put a stop to it right away.

"Yes?" I bark while keeping the phone between my ear and shoulder, and unbutton the green dress. Maybe it won't be so bad.

"Miss Grey," a deep voice answers, and the dress slips from my fingers. "I wanted to check if everything is going according to schedule on your side."

"Absolutely, Mr. Petrov. Why do you ask?"

"Because Maxim just called to tell me that you've been sitting in a changing room in some shop for almost an hour."

What? I grab the heavy curtain intending to march out of the changing room when I remember I'm in my underwear. Damn it!

"You're following me?" I whisper yell into the phone.

"Technically, Maxim is. I don't want to risk you disappearing without following through with our agreement."

I pick up the green dress from the floor and start putting

it on. "I'm not going anywhere. I'm trying to find a dress for your fucking party. Call off your stalker, Mr. Petrov."

Turning toward the mirror, I look at my reflection and groan. A big *no* for the green dress.

"You still don't have a dress? The party is in four hours."

"I know! But nothing here fits."

There is a pause on his side and then—"Stay there." The line goes dead.

What the fuck just happened? "Whatever." I mumble, staring at the phone, then collect the dresses and leave them with the sales assistant. There's one more shop I can check out in this part of the mall, but if I don't find something there, I have no idea what I'm going to do. I guess I could head to the upper level. There are a few upscale boutiques there. I might be able to find something, and they usually have a seamstress on-site who could shorten the dress right away. But, those shops are pricey. There is no way I am going to spend two grand on a dress.

I'm going toward the exit when I see the guy from the restaurant. I remember him standing a few paces behind Petrov the whole time. He's in his late forties and slightly overweight, but he carries it well. The dark suit and tie he's wearing are impeccable, definitely expensive. He looks like someone from a bank's upper management rather than a criminal. When I step out of the store, he sizes me up over his glasses and shakes his head. He probably finds me lacking. Like I give a fuck.

"Come on." He motions with his head toward the elevator. "They are waiting for you for the fitting."

"Who are 'they'?"

"The boutique staff."

"Which boutique?" I ask, entering the elevator.

"Roman said the most expensive one. I didn't pay attention to the name."

"I'm on a budget."

"Roman's paying."

I open my mouth to say no, then think about it. The guy is blackmailing me into marriage by dangling my father's life in front of my nose. He *should* be paying for the dress.

An hour and a half later, I exit the boutique with a huge garment bag concealing my new, professionally shortened dress, and two more boxes holding strappy heels and a clutch purse. I wonder what my future husband will think about my dress. One thing is certain, he won't like it when he sees the receipt.

Roman

She's late.

I return to the conversation around the table, doing my best to fake interest. I was never a fan of big gatherings. Fake people with fake smiles, pretending they are oh-so-happy to see you while, secretly, they wish for your demise. I look around the table and wonder which one of them set up the bomb that fucked up my life. It wasn't the Italians. Of that, I'm sure. This device was planted under my car, and if it were the Italians, they'd have rigged the whole warehouse. I was lucky the bastard got trigger happy and hit the remote a few seconds before I was inside. Only a handful of people knew my schedule for that day, and some of them are sitting at this table.

I reach for the whiskey bottle to refill my glass when my uncle lets out a whistle, like the uncivilized pig he is, and motions with his cigar toward the entrance.

"Nice ass," he comments.

I follow his gaze and my eyes land on a woman in a long emerald-green dress. Black embroidered decorations accentuate the neckline and her tiny waist, and then flow along the edges of a high slit, revealing one slender leg. My eyes trail the slit upward until they stop at her face, and I almost fail to recognize her. She's removed the nose ring. Her hair is different as well and is pulled up on the top of her head in some complicated design. I can hardly believe this is the same woman I met a few days earlier. The men at the table are mumbling between each other, and I wish they would shut up so I can enjoy the view in peace.

"Is that Samuel's wife?" someone asks.

"Yeah, right."

"Who is this Samuel guy?"

"He's handling the real estate purchases for Mikhail. It must be his daughter."

"Well, I wouldn't mind handling that for a night."

They continue laughing at their stupid jokes, and it makes me so mad I want to break their necks.

"Shut up," I bark and pin them, one by one, with my gaze.

They all stare at me for a second, and in the next moment, the conversation switches to another subject. I return to watching Nina. She's standing with her father and a few other men, smiling at something one of them said, and I feel this strange urge to shoot the man who's currently on the receiving end of her smile.

"See something you like, Roman?" My uncle nudges me with his shoulder.

"Maybe."

"She's a cute little thing. Not exactly your type."

"Leave." I reach for my drink. "And take the guys with you."

"What?"

"Go find another table, Leonid. Right now."

He mumbles something but stands, and a few moments later the other three chairs screech. I lean back in my wheelchair, letting my eyes go back to the little hellion on the other side of the room.

 Nina

There is a prickling feeling at the back of my neck. It started the moment we walked inside, and I can't shake it. It's probably anxiety from being here, in the middle of a wolf's den, surrounded by men and women in expensive outfits. They smile and chat, and I wonder how many of them have blood on their hands.

I turn to take a glass of wine from a waiter when my eyes land on the man sitting alone at the table in the corner and my heartbeat quickens.

Casually leaning back in his wheelchair, Petrov is watching me with narrowed eyes, and the vain part of me revels in his attention. Well yes, Mr. Petrov, I clean up nice. The night when we met, the gloomy restaurant's interior didn't allow me to see him clearly, but here, with all the grand chandeliers illuminating the room, I can finally see him in all his glory.

He's wearing black dress pants and a charcoal shirt with the two top buttons undone, revealing the ends of a black tattoo on his chest. The sleeves of his shirt are rolled up to his elbows, showing a similarly designed pattern around his right forearm. I'm not sure why, but he didn't strike me as a type of a man who'd ink his skin.

I've met many beautiful men. We even had a few fashion models come to pose for us in my Painting Practice Class. Their perfect facial features were always a challenge to replicate on paper. Roman Petrov isn't anything like those men, and comparing them would be like comparing a gazelle with a rabid tiger. They are a completely different species. If I had to pick one word to describe the Russian pakhan it would be devastating. Black hair a bit longer on the top, sharp cheekbones, and a nose slightly larger than perfect. Nothing that would stand out by itself, but together his is a face I'd never forget. Maybe it's his dark and piercing eyes, still focused on me, that give off that devilish vibe or his gaze that makes me want to turn around and bolt. It must be a primal reaction: the prey's unconscious knowledge of having been at the center of a predator's attention.

Without breaking eye contact, he reaches for the empty chair at his side, moves it closer to him, and nods toward it. I should probably go there, but my legs are rooted to the spot.

"Miss Grey, Roman Petrov is inviting you to join him," the man on my left says. "It's not wise to keep the pakhan waiting."

So, it looks like the show is on. With a deep breath, I plaster a seductive smile on my face and start walking toward, probably, the most dangerous man in the room. I wonder if I'm heading to my demise.

I stop right in front of him and offer him my hand. "Mr. Petrov, you called."

Instead of shaking it, he takes my fingers gently and lifts my hand to his lips, then places a soft kiss on my knuckles. It feels like fire just seared my flesh. He doesn't let go immediately, and I can't tear my eyes away, noticing how hilariously tiny my hand looks compared to his.

"Roman, please," he says in his deep baritone, and a flock of mad butterflies attack my insides.

I sit down next to him and quickly adjust the fabric of my dress to cover my trembling legs. When I throw a look toward my father, he's still standing with the same group of people, and every one of them is looking in our direction.

"It always works for you this way?" I ask, a fake smile plastered all over my face. "You pick a woman, nod, and she comes running?"

"Most of the time, yes."

"That must be fun."

"Not really." He takes a sip of his drink, watching the crowd milling around. Most of them are cutting glances at us, but when they catch Roman looking, they quickly turn their heads.

"Tell me, Nina, if there wasn't this deal between us, would you have come when I nodded?" he asks.

"Nope."

I don't expect him to ask me to elaborate, but he does, and his question surprises me. "Why not? Is it because of the wheelchair?"

He says it conversationally, but there is a hidden

undertone I can't quite define. I abandon watching the crowd and look him right in the eyes. "It's because I'm not a poodle, Mr. Petrov."

He laughs and takes another sip of his drink, shaking his head.

"What happened?" I nod toward his legs.

"You don't beat around the bush, do you, Nina?"

"Do you want me to?"

"It was a car bomb. Shrapnel hit my right knee and shattered it."

"Does it hurt?"

"Like a bitch," he says curtly and throws back the rest of his drink.

"You have money, I'm sure there's some surgery that would help."

"Well, it looks like there are things no amount of money can buy."

"Yeah. That sucks. At least you can buy a wife." I shrug. "For three million you could have gotten a whole harem, not just one."

Roman cocks his head to the side, observing me with interest, and then leans in to whisper in my ear. "You, Nina Grey, are one strange woman."

Even his voice is sexy, damn him.

"My mother thinks so, too. She says I'm never going to find a man who'd want to deal with my type of crazy—in the long run at least."

"What an optimistic, supportive parent." He reaches out with his hand and traces a line on the inside of my forearm, starting at the elbow down to the base of my palm. "Is there a boyfriend in the picture?"

It's almost impossible to concentrate while his finger continues tracing the line up and down my forearm. His touch is featherlight, but still, it feels like he's branding me. "Why do you ask? Would you reconsider releasing me from our contract if there was?"

"No."

"Then it doesn't matter, I guess."

Keeping his eyes on mine, he takes my hand in his and raises it to his lips, one corner of his mouth curving upward in a barely-there smile.

"I googled you yesterday," he says, still keeping my fingers in his hand, just an inch from his lips. "Who would have thought that such a delicate little hand could create such . . . disturbing art."

I smile, trying to hide how much his touch and nearness impact me. Roman Petrov, I've come to realize, is impossible to ignore, especially when he turns on the charm. "You don't like it?"

"Oh, on the contrary, Miss Grey. I love it."

His lips brush the tips of my fingers and stay there for a few seconds before he lowers my hand, but he keeps holding it in his. He's playing his part so well, this devious, dangerous man.

"Would you paint something for me?"

I look up at him, surprised by his question. "I don't do commissions."

"Any particular reason?"

"I don't like to be pressed into doing things I don't want to do."

Roman's lips widen in a smile. Yup, he understood the double meaning.

"How about a trade, then? You paint something for me, and I give you something you want."

"Anything?"

"Money, jewelry, anything you want."

Tempting. It's not a thing that I want from him, though. "I want an answer to a question," I say. "Is that an option as well?"

My choice surprises him. I see it in the way his eyes widen slightly. And he's not happy. "Depends on the question."

"In that case, I'll have to decline, Mr. Petrov."

He looks at me and then bursts out laughing, making several heads turn in our direction. "You drive a hard bargain, Miss Grey." He leans his head and whispers in my ear, "Ask."

I find it hard to believe that he's accepted. Petrov doesn't seem like a man who would agree to anyone's terms. He must really want that painting. I lift my head and look into his calculating dark eyes, while several possibilities run through my head.

"Why do you need a temporary wife, Roman? You're handsome, rich, powerful. I'm sure there are dozens of women who'd be happy to marry you. Why waste three million dollars when you could get a wife for free?"

"Because I don't want a permanent one, and the current business situation requires me to have a wife for the next six months."

"Why six months?"

"Well, that's a second question." He smiles. "And you bargained for only one."

Touché.

He answered without revealing anything at all. I should've expected it and phrased my question differently, but there's no going back now.

"So, what do you want me to paint for you? A landscape? Your dog? Apples, cheese, and dead flowers on a table?" Those are the usual requests when it comes to custom commissions, and the main reason why I hate doing them.

"Nope. I had something else in mind." There it is again, that devious calculating half-smile. "I want your self-portrait."

"A self-portrait?" I raise my eyebrows. What the hell is he going to do with my self-portrait? Why not a landscape?

"Yes. Is that a problem?"

"No. Any special requests? Pose? Background?"

He leans forward until his face is looming right in front of mine, takes my chin with two fingers, and tilts my head up a little.

"Just one," he says and focuses his gaze on my lips. "I want you to be naked."

My eyes widen at the realization of what he just said, and I'm so stunned that I can't find a meaningful response.

"It looks like we've become a main attraction in the room," he murmurs, still focused on my lips. "Are you ready, Nina?"

His nearness is doing funny things to my already unsettled mind, and dear God, he smells amazing. Trying to get back down to earth, I start chanting a new mantra in my head: *He's a criminal. He's a criminal.*

"Ready? For . . . what?" I mumble.

"To show me how good an actress you really are." He smiles and crashes his lips to mine.

Erased. Every single coherent thought vaporized. One second, I'm a thinking rational being. The next, every single logical thought vanishes, only to be replaced with one

30

maddening need—more. More of his lips, more of his smell, more of everything.

There is a sound of a glass shattering. Something wet splashes my feet. I open my eyes and start registering the reality piece by piece. Roman's face is looming just an inch from mine, his hand is on the back of my neck. My fingers are in his hair, clutching the silky black strands.

"That was an outstanding performance," he says in low voice. "The glass was a masterful detail."

I remove my hands from Roman's hair and look down where my wine glass lays shattered in pieces. Red liquid mares the pristine white marble floor, and some of it has splashed all over my right foot and shoe.

Roman grabs the wheels on his chair and in two quick motions repositions himself so he is in front of me. "Swap your legs, Miss Grey. Right one up."

Regarding him through narrowed eyes, I uncross my legs, then cross them again so my right one is crossed over the left.

He bends, wraps his hand around my right ankle, undoes the clasp, and slips the strap from my heel. He removes the shoe, and I stare at his hands as he wipes the wine from my foot with a white napkin he's taken from the table. When he's done, he puts my heel back on and closes the clasp. Holding my ankle, he slowly lowers my leg back down.

I'm only partially aware of the people in the room who have gone unusually quiet—every one of them staring at us. I'm trying and failing to process what's just happened. It's the most erotic nonsexual thing I've ever experienced.

"I think it's time for us to leave," Roman says and motions with his hand toward Maxim who's leaning on the wall not far from us. "Go to your father, tell him you're coming with me, and make sure a few people hear you say it. We'll be waiting in the car at the front."

He takes the wheels of his chair and guides it toward the exit with Maxim following him a few paces behind. People watch them leave, and then their eyes focus on me. I feel like I'm on display as I walk to my father and kiss him on the cheek. "Roman has asked me to join him for a private drink."

Whispers break out around us. Father smiles, but it's forced, so I pat him on the arm before I cross the hall toward the exit. The crowd's eyes bore into my back. They probably think I'm a slut, but I don't give a damn. With my head held high and a fake smile on my lips, I leave the room.

There's a big white car in the front as promised. Maxim is standing by the back door and opens it for me when I approach. As I get inside, I can't help but wonder what the hell I am doing.

I knew Roman was rich. He had to be, with him being the head of the Bratva, so I assumed he would live in some grand house. What I'm currently looking at, though, is not a house. It's a damn fortress, and it comes with its own small army.

Tall concrete walls surround a huge estate on all four sides, and cameras are mounted on the top at every ten feet. The car drives through a big automatic gate with a guardhouse on the side and follows a wide gravel road to a monstrosity of a mansion. A perfectly manicured lawn stretches all around, and there are only a few scattered trees placed here and there so they don't obstruct the view. Security measure probably.

Two men in black gear with guns on their belts are positioned in front of the house, and a few more patrol the grounds. I'm sure there are more I can't see.

"Do you have cameras inside as well?" I ask.

"If you want people to trust you and stay loyal, you have to reciprocate," Roman says from next to me. "Placing the cameras inside would mean I don't trust my men."

The car stops at the front of the house and Maxim opens the door for me while the driver goes to the trunk to take out Roman's wheelchair. I exit the car and look over the building. It's only two stories high, but it expands at least fifty yards on each side. The thing is gigantic.

Roman rolls up beside me. "You like it?"

"No."

"Why?"

"I'm not a fan of large things," I mumble.

Three stone steps lead to the main door, and I wonder how Roman will get up them, but then I notice a narrow ramp at the far side. He wheels himself up with ease. Watching him, I feel a pang of sadness. It must be hard for a man like him to have his life turned upside down so drastically. I take the steps to meet him at the entrance, and a security guard awaiting Roman's arrival opens the big oak door for us.

Roman leads me across the big foyer to the elevator under a huge double stairway. A man in the same black gear as those outside enters from the hallway on the left. When he sees us, he stops and nods his head to Roman.

"Pakhan," he says.

"Is Varya still awake?"

"Yes. I think she's in the kitchen."

"Tell her I'm back. Have her instruct one of the girls to

prepare a quick dinner and then she can go to bed," Roman says and gazes at me. "And tell the staff to make sure to stay out of the east wing. I don't want anyone there unless I call for them."

"For tonight?"

I see a mysterious smile form on Roman's lips. "No. Tell them it's until further notice, Vova. I'll ring the kitchen when we're ready for dinner."

"Of course." The man nods and turns to leave, but not before he glances in my direction with interest.

Judging by his facial expression and the way his eyes widened after Roman's remark, the gossip is about to begin.

When we exit the elevator, Roman leads me down the hallway on the left and through the ornate wooden door opening into a huge space with a living room in the center. There's a library on the far left and an enormous modern kitchen with a dining room on the right. The furniture is sparse, I guess to make it easier for him to get around. The space is decorated in earth tones, mostly browns and beige, with lots of natural material—wood, mostly. It's modern, but not cold. I like it.

"We need to go through some basics," he says and nods toward the living area where a long sofa that could probably sit five people takes the central place in front of the big TV mounted on the wall.

"You will be sleeping in the room over there." He points to the right. "My bedroom is on the other side."

The space is so huge it takes me a few seconds to locate the doors he's talking about. I don't particularly care how the room looks, as long as it has a soft bed and a keyed lock on the door. My feet are killing me, so I go toward the sofa, taking off my heels along the way, and drop down onto soft cushions.

It feels strange, being here in his space. I'm going to be living here for the next six months. With him. Somehow it all seemed unreal until this moment, as if everything was happening to someone else. But now, with me sitting on his sofa, in his house, it finally hits me. This is really happening.

I should be fucking scared. Something must be very wrong with me because, yes, I feel the anxiety and I'm nervous, but there is no fear. I look up to meet the eyes of the head of the Russian criminal underworld—the man who promised to kill me if I fail to play my part in his strange scheme—and that flock of butterflies explodes in my stomach again. Dear God, I need to have my head checked, because instead of being afraid like a normal person, I'm attracted to him.

 Roman

"It's late, so I'll walk you through the house tomorrow." I wheel myself toward the sofa. "It would be best if you don't roam around alone until I introduce you to everyone."

"Okay." Nina nods. "So, what now?"

"I'll call the kitchen to bring us some food since we didn't eat anything. Do you want something specific?"

"I'm not hungry, but it wouldn't hurt to let the staff walk in on us. It'll make the gossip pick up pace."

Doing a show for the staff wasn't in my plan for tonight. I assumed she'd want to go to bed to get away from me as soon as we arrived, but now I'm curious about what she has in mind. It's slightly disturbing—the way she acts is so casual, like this whole situation is completely normal. There is nothing normal about being pressured to move in with a stranger and pose as his wife. She must really love her father to agree to this sham and be so invested.

While I'm calling the kitchen, Nina starts taking out the pins from her hair, and I watch the long black strands fall down her back one by one, like a waterfall of inky silk. I wonder if her hair is as soft as it looks.

"When do you expect the maid to arrive?" Nina asks as she takes out the last pin.

"Any second."

"Okay then, let's start." She gets up from the sofa and comes to stand before me.

Leaning in, she starts undoing the buttons on my shirt, her face the embodiment of calm, but I notice that her hands are shaking slightly. A normal reaction, at last. When she's done with my shirt, she cocks her head like she's thinking about something and then looks me in the eyes.

"Can I hop on?"

I narrow my eyes. "Where?"

"In your lap? Will it hurt your leg?"

She wants to climb into my lap? I can't stop staring at her. "It won't hurt my leg."

Nina nods, pulls her dress up with one hand, and places the other on my shoulder. Then she bites her bottom lip, obviously confused on where to go from there. I lean in, grab her around the waist and hoist her up to deposit her across my thighs. She yelps, her arms going around my neck and her eyes widen.

"And now what?" I ask, trying to stifle a laugh.

"Now we wait for the maid to catch us cuddling."

"But we're not doing that, are we? You're just sitting in

my lap." Reaching with my hand, I move a long black strand of hair that's fallen over her face, then holding her at the nape, lean in and place a kiss on her slender neck. With my other hand I find the slit of her dress and hear her sharp intake of breath when I start moving my fingers up her naked thigh.

A knock comes from the door.

"Enter!" I bark over Nina's shoulder and then resume trailing kisses along her neck.

"Pakhan, Varya said to bring—" Valentina's voice cuts off in the middle of the sentence.

"Leave the tray in the kitchen and be gone." My words are sharp, as if Valentina is interrupting something real. My body seems to think so.

The girl hurries to leave the food and then literally runs off, banging the door behind her.

As soon as Valentina is gone, Nina lets go of my neck, and hastily hops off my lap. Good. If she stayed there any longer she'd probably notice my hard dick straining against the material of my pants.

"So, that went well, I guess," she says and passes her hands through her hair, only making it more tangled.

"A lovely performance indeed."

"Well, I'd better go to bed now." She starts toward the door of her room but stops midway. "Can I borrow a shirt or something?" She throws the question over her shoulder. "I don't want to sleep in Oscar de la Renta."

The idea of her in my clothes does something to my insides, and I imagine grabbing her and taking her to my bed. I don't like that at all. This is a business deal and nothing else. "I'll bring you something. We can send someone to get your things tomorrow, leave your keys in the kitchen."

 Nina

After a quick shower, I put on the gray T-shirt Roman left on the door handle for me, get in the large four-poster bed and snuggle under the comforter. I checked the time on my phone before getting into bed. It's well after midnight, but I can't sleep. Being in a strange house is just part of the reason. A much larger part is sleeping a couple of dozen yards away. Just thinking about him is messing with my already fried brain.

Roman's chest is fully covered with ink. I saw it when I unbuttoned his shirt, but there wasn't enough time for me to pay much attention to the designs. I wish I did, because this need to reveal at least some of his secrets is eating me from the inside. The Russian pakhan is an enigma, and the complete opposite of the straightforward funny guys—ones who can make me laugh—I'm usually attracted to. I like a carefree spirit, someone who is easy to talk to and even easier to leave—a man who won't demand me to open up. Getting tangled up with the pakhan any more than strictly necessary for this plan to work is not wise.

I close my eyes and the image of Roman gripping my thigh while his sinful lips trail a line of kisses down my neck fills my mind. As if on its own accord, my hand slides down my stomach and stops between my legs. I place a finger at my core, press lightly, and groan. No. I should not be pleasuring myself while thinking of a man who threatened to kill me. It's so wrong. Quickly, I remove my hand, tuck both under the pillow, and try to ignore the ache between my legs. I am not doing this.

For hours I lie awake in bed, clutching the pillow with my fingers, waiting for my traitorous body to calm itself. It doesn't. In fact, it only gets worse until I can't take it anymore, so I finally succumb to my need and slide my hand back down between my legs. I come in a matter of seconds, with my face buried in the pillow and the name of a killer on my lips.

Chapter
four

M Y PHONE RINGS WHILE I'M BUTTONING MY shirt, showing my uncle's name on the screen. The old boar normally likes to sleep till noon on Sundays. I know only one reason why he would be calling this early.

"What is it, Leonid?" I bark into the phone.

"I heard you brought a woman. Is she still at the house?"

"This is my house, so it doesn't concern you."

"That means she is. You never bring your sluts home," he says, and my body goes rigid.

"If I hear you call her that again, in front of me or anyone else, I'm going to slit your throat. Is that clear?"

"What the hell has gotten into you, Roman?"

"Have I been clear, Leonid?"

There is silence on the other side of the line before he answers, "Yes."

"Good." I cut the line.

I hate that man, but I can't risk throwing him out, no

matter how much I want to. Leonid knows too much, and I need him here, where I can keep my eye on him the whole time.

I reach for the crutches leaning on the nightstand, place them on either side of me, and hoist myself up. Putting the crutches under my armpits, I take a deep breath and make the first few painfully slow steps. My knee is usually stiff in the mornings, but it's much better than it was a month ago. All those hours of physical therapy are finally paying off, but I'm still a long way away from getting rid of the damn wheelchair. I hate the damn thing, but I still have days when the pain is too strong, and I can't bear to even move my right leg.

When I find the bastards who planted that bomb, I'm going to enjoy killing them. I might have been sedated, but I remember two people talking in my hospital room. I couldn't recognize the voices or grasp the whole meaning of what was said, but I understood enough to know they were involved.

One of them is probably my flesh and blood, living under my roof. I don't have proof, but I'm almost certain that Leonid played a part. Who is the other one? I still have to find out.

When I leave my room, I hear a sound of slightly off-key singing coming from the kitchen and turn to see Nina rummaging through the fridge. I knew she was short, but from my sitting position last night, I wasn't able to pinpoint her exact height. She's even shorter than I thought, barely five feet. The hem of my T-shirt reaches down to her knees, and she looks comical in it. Barefoot, the top of her head wouldn't even come to my breastbone.

She's standing with her back to me, so she doesn't see me when I approach and stand by the dining table a few paces behind her.

"Anything interesting in that fridge?" I ask.

Nina jumps with a startled yelp and closes the fridge with a bang. "Shit, you almost gave me a heart att—"

She stops mid-sentence and just stands there staring at me, her eyes huge. I expected her to be surprised seeing me out of the wheelchair, but the emotion showing on her face is not a surprise. It's fear.

"Nina?" I take a step toward her.

She flinches and takes a step back, bumping into the fridge. Her breathing quickens, becoming shallow like she can't take enough air in, and her hands are slightly trembling. She's having a panic attack. I have no idea what's triggered it, but she's terrified of something and I'm pretty certain that *something* is me. It makes no sense. Just a few hours earlier I was holding her in my lap, and she didn't look scared at all.

"Roman," she says finally, her voice barely above a whisper, "I need you to sit down. Please."

I don't see the sense in her request, but I take two steps toward the dining table, pull out the chair, and sit down. Nina stays rooted to the spot in front of the fridge, but at least her breathing seems to be coming under control.

A stray thought crosses my mind, something she said when we arrived. I remember it clearly now and I don't like what it implies. "You said something last night. I need you to explain what you meant by that."

She blinks and shakes her head. "What exactly?"

Her voice is stronger now, almost normal, but still, she doesn't move. Her back is plastered to the fridge like she wants to melt into it.

I focus my eyes on her face, making sure I catch her reaction. "What did you mean by 'I'm not a fan of large things'?"

She blinks and, instead of answering, turns on her heel and runs into her room. The door closes with a bang at the same time my realization settles in and anger starts boiling in my stomach. Someone hurt her, and for her to react this way, it must have been really bad.

 Nina

The clock on the nightstand shows two p.m. I can't stay locked in the room the whole day, I know that. But still, I can't make myself go out there and face Roman after the episode from this morning. He probably thinks I'm crazy. God, even after two years, I'm still fucked up in the head.

It was getting better. I came to a point where I was able to be in the company of huge men without freaking out. I could even hold a normal conversation, as long as they didn't touch me. Yes, most people, especially men, are taller than me. But most of them don't trigger a panic attack. I only react to men who are as tall as Brian had been, and who have significant muscle mass.

Roman looks nothing like Brian, who was blond and had a surfer look about him, but they are of similar height and build. Maybe if I was warned in some way, or if I knew what to expect, I wouldn't have reacted so extremely. But I was still sleepy, and with Roman suddenly towering in front of me, I just flipped.

I have to get out of this room. There is still work to do, people to deceive. I can do this.

Lifted by my pep talk, I get up from the bed, and with my head held high, I march out of the room.

Roman is sitting at the table, fork in one hand and holding his phone to his ear with the other. Judging by the dark look on his face, it's not good news. I do my best to school my features and join him, picking the chair next to him on purpose. My action says, "I'm not afraid of you. The episode from the kitchen was just a misunderstanding. Let's pretend it never happened."

He's still on the phone when I sit down, but he's been following my every step with his eyes. Making sure that my moves are perfectly calm, I fill a glass with water and focus on the food in the middle of the table. There's a bowl of mashed potatoes, an assortment of fish, and some salads, so I take a plate and pile it up. I grab a slice of bread as well and dig in.

"I'll be downstairs in twenty minutes," Roman says into the phone, puts it down on the table, and resumes eating.

We eat in silence, the only sound coming from the cutlery and it's strangely . . . domestic. I expect him to start asking about this morning, but he doesn't mention it, and I'm relieved.

"I sent Valentina to pick up some of your clothes," he says finally. "They're in a bag in the living room."

"Peachy." I grab a cherry tomato from my plate and throw it in my mouth.

Roman leans back and, crossing his arms in front of him, watches me for a few seconds. I try to focus on my food instead of his muscular arms which are stretching the material of his shirt. I fail miserably.

He tilts his head to the side and narrows his eyes at me.

"You know, I find it very interesting that you are handling this situation much better than I hoped."

"What situation?" I reach for the salad bowl and refill my plate with lettuce and more cherry tomatoes.

"This. Being blackmailed into a marriage with someone like me. Having to put your life on hold for six months. I expected you to be wary. Reluctant. Scared. You seem . . . unnaturally nonchalant."

"You think I'm mentally unstable?" I take a leaf of lettuce, wrap it around a cherry tomato and dip it into the mayonnaise while Roman regards me with interest.

"Are you?" he asks. "Mentally unstable?"

"Of course, not. I'm the embodiment of mental stability. Ask anyone." I point to my lettuce-tomato-mayo ball. "You want one?"

Based on the look on his face, he is not amused. I sigh and look him straight in the eyes. "Yes, I find this situation disturbing, but it is what it is. Do I have a say in it? No. Can I change anything? Again, no. Whether I fight it or not, the result will be the same. The way I see it, it's better to just accept the fucking thing and go along with it."

"You're a little nuts, you know that, right?"

"Life is crazy. You have to embrace it." I shrug and motion with my head toward the crutches leaned on the table next to him. "Why the wheelchair when you can walk?"

"I'd rather call it dragging. And I still can't manage the whole day on crutches. I plan on ditching the wheelchair at some point, but until I can make it a full day, I don't want anyone to know."

"Why not?"

"I have my reasons. Only Maxim, Varya, and my

physiotherapist know. And now you. I want to keep it that way, Nina."

"Nobody has caught you walking? A maid? Someone coming into your suite unannounced?"

"Only Varya is allowed in here. She handles the cleaning. Everyone else knows to stay out of my suite unless they are specifically invited."

"And what would happen if someone did catch you? Would that be a problem?"

"Not really. Because I would kill them on the spot."

At first, I think he's joking, but then he looks at me and I see it in his eyes. He's deadly serious.

"You're a scary man, Mr. Petrov."

"It goes with the job description, Nina," he says. "There are only three things people understand in my world: loyalty, money, and death. Remember that." He reaches for the crutches. "I have to discuss something with Maxim. I'll be back in an hour."

I stand up quickly, take a deep breath, and will my legs not to move from the spot. There's no way I'll allow the episode from this morning to repeat itself. He's not Brian. I will not let my unreasonable fear rule me.

Roman positions his crutches on either side of him and stands upright in front of me. Dear God, he's huge. My heartbeat quickens but I manage not to flinch. I can handle this. I'll be living with him for the next six months, so I have to get it together. Very slowly I raise my head and look him in the eyes without batting an eyelash. But I sure as hell make certain my trembling hands are hidden behind my back.

"I wonder what they fed you growing up," I say, and even manage a small smirk.

He just watches me for a few seconds, and then reaches with his hand and trails his thumb down my cheek.

"You are an exceptional actress, malysh."

His hand vanishes from my cheek, and he slowly heads into his bedroom. I wonder what he meant by that.

CHAPTER
five

 Roman

I LOOK BLANKLY AT MAXIM, WHO IS STANDING IN FRONT of my desk with his arms crossed at his chest, wondering where he's getting his stupid ideas from all of a sudden.

"No," I say.

"Why not? It's a perfect opportunity. She can say she just got lost or she's exploring the house."

"Because one, she probably never saw a listening device in her life and wouldn't know how or where to place it. And two, no one will believe that she just wandered into Leonid's room or his office by accident. We don't know who else is involved. Could be someone from the staff or one of the security guys. I don't want her tipping off Leonid or his partner sooner than intended."

"You're sure it was Leonid?"

"Very."

"Let's just bag him right away then. Get Mikhail to work on him. He'll be singing like a bird by morning."

"And if it wasn't him?" I ask. "Do you have any idea how

it would impact the morale and trust of my men if I tortured one of my own without proof, only to have him turn out innocent?"

"Well, then we have reached a dead-end, Roman." He takes off his glasses and sighs, "I've been listening to the recordings for months and didn't find anything other than standard gossip. Did you know that Kostya is sleeping with both Valentina and Olga?"

"I don't give a damn who is sleeping with whom. Which rooms have you bugged so far?"

"The library, the lounge, dining room, both downstairs bathrooms, the basement, and armory as well. Varya bugged the kitchen and the pantry for me. That's it."

"The cars?"

"All except Leonid's, Mikhail's, and Sergei's."

"You don't have to bug Sergei's car. If he'd been the one who set up that bomb, I would be dead. Together with the whole damn block probably. It's not Mikhail either." I tap my finger on the desk, thinking. "Have Valentina place a bug in Leonid's room and his office."

"Valentina?"

"Why not? She can be trusted."

He shakes his head. "Well, let me put it this way. Last night, Nina was sitting on your lap, with her hair in disarray, barefoot, clutching her arm around your neck as you were groping her leg under her dress. Your shirt was unbuttoned, and you were kissing her like a man possessed," Maxim says and raises his eyebrows at me. "The whole staff knew every single detail the moment Valentina rushed back to the kitchen, as well as her conclusion that you two are soul mates and will have beautiful babies soon. She's loyal, but her tongue is a mile long. There is no way she can keep her mouth shut even if her life depended on it."

"Fucking great." I take a deep breath and look at the ceiling. Is there anyone in this household who is even remotely sane?

"We should get Nina to do it. The staff and the men still haven't met her, and if you instruct her to pose like a giggly, simple-minded idiot, no one will pay attention to what she's doing."

"I would never marry a 'giggly simple-minded idiot', Maxim. Everyone knows that."

"Of course, you would. You're a man possessed, remember?"

I close my eyes and shake my head in irritation. One of these days, I'm going to strangle Valentina.

"That's settled then." Maxim straightens his jacket, puts his glasses on, and turns to leave. "Let me know when you want me to come and explain the procedure to Nina."

When I get back to my suite in the east wing, I don't see Nina anywhere—not in the kitchen nor the living room—so I head to her bedroom, which I find empty as well. For a moment I think she's changed her mind and somehow got away. I turn my wheelchair, planning on raising the alarm, when I notice her, and the pressure I didn't realize was gripping my chest vanishes.

She is sitting cross-legged in the farthest corner of the library with her back to the bookshelf, a bunch of paper towels spread on the floor around her. I wheel myself across the living room, stop a few paces away, and watch. She's sketching something on one of the paper towels. It's very basic, but I can see the shape of a woman holding something in front of her. Most of the other paper towels scattered around bear similar compositions; some are just unrecognizable lines, others more detailed. I couldn't have been gone more than an hour. How did she manage to do all that in such a short time?

"Can you send someone to my place to bring my things?" Nina asks without removing her eyes from the drawing. "There are three large boxes in the living room. Tell them to be careful, my canvases and paints are inside."

"When do you need them?"

"Yesterday. Since I'm stuck here, I better do something useful with my time. I have the exhibition in three weeks, and I only have six pieces done. I need nine more, as well as the big guy."

"The 'big guy'?"

"My main piece. I ordered the canvas for that one, it'll arrive next week."

I watch her work a few more minutes, noticing the way she narrows her eyes on some detail from time to time, or how she cocks her head to the side and bites her cheek when she's thinking. Her hair is a mess of tangled strands which she's collected at the top of her head and fixed with a pencil. Such a strange creature. So different from the women I'm used to spending my time with. It's refreshing, and dangerously alluring.

"I need to talk to you when you're done," I say when I manage to take my eyes off her. "I'll be in the living room."

"Yup." She places the finished sketch on the side, takes the last unused paper towel, and starts drawing on it.

It looks like I'm being dismissed.

After making a trip to my bedroom to grab the laptop I keep there, I transfer myself to the sofa and turn on the news. I prop my right leg on the table in front of me, open the laptop, and start going through the emails. I'm almost done when Nina drops down next to me and yawns.

"Sorry, I got carried away. What did you want to talk about?"

I close the laptop and turn to face her. "I need you to do something for me while you're here."

"Like vacuum and dust?" She scrunches her nose. "I don't remember agreeing to that. Ironing is okay, dusting as well, but I hate vacuuming."

"To place some bugs here in the house, without anyone noticing."

She looks at me with a mix of confusion and disgust on her face, so it seems I have to clarify. "Listening devices. Not insects."

"That is a really strange request, Mr. Petrov. Care to elaborate?"

"It's Roman from now on. Please make sure you don't slip when someone is around."

"I won't slip, Roman." She smiles and winks at me. She fucking winks at me.

I sigh. "I have reason to believe that at least one of the people who organized the bomb meant to kill me is here in this house. Maxim covered most of the rooms with bugs two months ago, but he can't place them in the last few without risking someone seeing him."

"Well, I'm touched by your belief in my capabilities, but I really can't see how I'm going to manage that if he couldn't."

"Because if anyone saw Maxim entering any of those rooms, they'll know something's not right. But if anyone catches you, you can always say that you got lost."

"Your house is huge, but I don't think that I would get so lost as to enter the wrong room." She looks offended. "I'm not an idiot."

"That brings us to the second thing we need to discuss, and it concerns how people who live and work here perceive you. I need you to appear . . . let's say shallow."

"You mean stupid?"

"Not exactly. What I need is that, when people see you entering the room, they aren't wary or suspicious. I want them to secretly roll their eyes and not notice what you're doing, because they assume you're . . . harmless."

She watches me in surprise, then laughs. It's an unguarded and genuine laugh which reaches her eyes. "Okay, you definitely mean stupid. Okay. I'll need a few minutes."

She leans back into the cushions, throws her head back, and with her face turned up toward the ceiling, she closes her eyes. She stays like that for a few moments and then starts speaking.

"Shallow. Harmless. A little bit stupid. Crazy in love with you, of course. Needs access to every part of the house. Let's see . . . Who am I? Well, Roman's trophy wife, of course. I am pretty, elegant, and extremely snobbish. I love wearing expensive clothes, just the best labels. I'm not really into dresses unless the occasion requires it. I much more prefer designer jeans, paired with silky blouses. The heels are a must."

She pauses, opens her eyes, and turns toward me.

"Are heels a must, do you think?" She scrunches her tiny nose. "Of course, they are. Damn it. I hate wearing heels."

She closes her eyes again and continues.

"The heels are a must, and I have dozens of them. Roman loves when I wear them, he says they make my butt look amazing. I'm also very self-conscious about my height and wearing heels all the time makes me forget how short I am. My favorite pastime is shopping, and I buy a ton of clothes. My husband has to allocate one driver specifically for me and my shopping sprees."

Another pause and she turns toward me again.

"Roman, I'll need funds to support her addiction with clothes. She is an impulse buyer."

"You'll get anything you need," I laugh. She's completely nuts.

"My husband is crazy about me, and he allows me to do whatever I want with the house, like rearrange furniture, so the vibe of the house works better with the earth vibrations. The house feels terribly cold, so I buy a bunch of indoor plants and spread them everywhere. I also tour every single room because I want to make sure the unobstructed energy flows, so I rearrange paintings and mirrors. I also hate the dining room table, it's so overstated and I decide to swap it with a sleek glass one I found in an interior design magazine."

Another pause.

"This woman is expensive, Roman. I hope you know what you're getting yourself into."

"I'll manage."

"Your funeral." She shrugs and continues. "My husband doesn't like it when he's interrupted, but of course, that doesn't apply to me. I often come into his office just to check up on him and exchange a few kisses. It annoys his men so much. They wonder what he sees in me and why he allows me so much freedom, and then decide he's thinking with his dick. I'm always around, and they hate it."

I'm fascinated with the way she's creating this new person. It's both crazy and brilliant. "She must be amazing in bed, to be able to wrap her husband around her finger that way," I comment.

"Of course, she is. How else would she make him lose his mind like that? She's not very bright, but she gives the best blowjobs."

I imagine Nina doing just that, and my dick gets instantly hard.

She opens her eyes and pins me with her gaze. "I guess that's enough for the start, I'll develop her more along the way. What do you think? Would she do?"

"Do you do this often? Create different personalities and slide into them," I ask, trying to suppress the need to grab her and kiss her silly.

"I did when I was a kid. It was a game. My mom hated it. Imagine having your daughter come down one morning and reject the breakfast, declaring that she's been a vegetarian for years when she just had ham and eggs for dinner the previous day. She yawns again. "Would you mind if I go take a nap? I didn't sleep well last night."

"Why?"

Nina blinks, looks the other way, and jumps from the sofa. "The bed was too soft."

I watch her as she runs to her bedroom and wonder why her cheeks reddened.

Nina

When I leave my room after my nap, I find an older woman standing in Roman's kitchen, putting groceries into the fridge. She's short with gray hair, wearing a classy yellow dress. When she hears me, she turns and smiles widely, which makes the wrinkles in the corners of her eyes stand out.

"I was wondering where you were," she says with a heavy accent. "The kitchen has been bursting with gossip since last night."

"Nina, this is Varya," Roman says entering the kitchen. "Varya knows about our agreement."

The older woman looks me over, from the top of my head and down to my toes, making me feel like I'm sixteen and meeting my boyfriend's mom for the first time. This woman is important to Roman, it's evident from the sound of his voice when he talks to her. He seems less guarded, somehow. If he shared the truth about our deal with her, it means he trusts her, and I don't think that Roman trusts many people.

"So, when's the wedding planned for?" she asks.

"In a few weeks." I shrug.

"I don't think that's a good idea, Roman." Varya turns to him. "If you keep Nina here that long, you'll have to introduce her to your men. I'm not sure it's a good idea to introduce her as your . . . lover."

"You think we should do it sooner?" he asks.

"Yes. When you take her to your men, it should be as your wife. No one will respect her otherwise."

Roman watches Varya for a few moments, then takes his phone and makes a call.

"Maxim, change of plans. Reschedule the marriage official. For tomorrow afternoon."

Whoa, what?

"That's much better." Varya smiles. "When should I send dinner?"

"In an hour."

"Perfect. I'll make sure it's Valentina who brings it, she described the scene she walked into yesterday with such detail. Very talented tattletale, that one. The whole kitchen staff and some of the men who were present listened to her with wide eyes, commenting how you never bring women to your home and how special this one must be." Varya turns to leave but stops at the door. "Make sure she catches you doing something more intimate this time. You don't want people to become suspicious when you announce that you two got married so suddenly, Roman."

I stare at the door that Varya just went through, confused and slightly panicked, then turn to Roman. "We are not having sex so that your maid can catch us."

He laughs and heads toward his bedroom. "I'm going to take a shower and change. If you plan on doing the same, be quick and put on something lacy."

"Excuse me?"

"There won't be any sex involved. But Valentina will be

bringing dinner to my room, and you are going to be there." He throws the words over his shoulder.

"In your room?"

"In my bed, Nina."

Roman

I'm rummaging through the kitchen drawer looking for a corkscrew when I hear the door to Nina's room open. I lift my head and stare. Nina is standing in the doorway looking like some dark princess in a short lacy nightgown, with her midnight hair falling free on either side of her face.

She enters the kitchen on bare feet and comes to stand right in front of me, but she keeps her head down looking at my feet. On the outside she seems relaxed, but then she looks up and her back goes rigid. So, it's like I assumed, it's not being close to me that bothers her. It's my height.

I remove the left crutch from under my armpit to lean it against the kitchen island, bend to grab Nina around her waist, and lift her to sit onto the counter in front of me.

"There. Better?" I ask, but she only stares at me with wide eyes.

I turn to retrieve the left crutch from behind me and when I face her again, I see a stray tear trailing down her face. The sight guts me.

"I'm sorry," she whispers. "It's not you, Roman."

"I know." I reach out to place my palm on her cheek and brush away the tear. "I'm going to kill him, malysh. It's going to be slow, and it's going to be painful. Just give me his name."

"No."

"I'm not asking. Give me his fucking name."

"I said no. I'm not making anyone a murderer."

"Too late for that, Nina. The name."

"Leave it. I'm not telling you. Just . . . leave it, damn it."

I take a deep breath and try to bottle up the need to smash my hand into something.

"Okay. I'll leave it for now. But you're just delaying the inevitable."

The phone starts ringing in my bedroom. It's probably Varya checking to see if we're ready for dinner, but I'm not in the mood for playing games anymore.

"I have to get that." I turn to walk toward the bedroom and hear Nina getting down from the counter.

She follows, keeping herself a few steps behind me, matching my slow pace. The phone stops ringing just as I reach the nightstand.

"I'll tell Varya that the tray must be left in front of the door." I say as I lower myself to sit on the edge of the bed. "You can go back to your room or wait in the kitchen."

"No." She reaches for the crutches I leaned next to me and slides them under the bed. I watch as she removes the bedcover and gets under the blanket.

"Come on," she says, lifting the corner of the blanket.

Making sure there is enough space between us, I lie down expecting her to stay back. Instead, she throws her leg around me and climbs on top, lowering her head to place it on my chest. I barely breathe, trying my best not to move even a muscle, afraid of spooking her. We stay like that for a few moments, me lying still with her sprawled over my chest.

"Put your arms around me."

I do as she says, watching for any sign of distress, but there isn't any. What an unusual creature she is, and it feels so good to hold her in my arms like this. I wish it wasn't just for show.

"Is this okay?" I rasp.

"Yup," she says and closes her eyes. "I need to give you a few pointers."

"All right."

"No holding my wrists or squeezing my neck." She says, and I feel the cold rush down my spine. "Also, no pinning me down with your body."

 Nina

The moment the words leave my mouth, Roman goes still under me. I hate speaking about this, but I had to tell him. I don't want to risk freaking out on him if he unknowingly did some of those things. He just lies there, and I hear his heart-beat quicken under my ear, and then he removes his arms from my back.

"Go back to your room, malysh. We are not doing this," he says in a clipped tone.

Shit. I knew he would react this way.

"It's okay, Roman."

"No. You've been hurt. I'm not going to make you—"

"You're not making me do anything." I raise my head to look at him, then crawl up until my face is right in front of his.

"Nina—" he starts, but I quickly put my finger over his lips.

"I had sex . . . after. I have no problem with being in the same bed as you. I won't freak out if you're holding me, or from being close to you."

His lips are so soft, and for a moment I'm distracted by the sight of him watching me with such intensity. He's so beautiful.

"It never came to that," I continue. "He . . . he never got to hurt me that way. I smashed his laptop into his head before he managed to do anything."

"You hit his head with a laptop."

"Twice. Broke his nose with the second blow and ran away." I shrug and run my finger over Roman's eyebrow. "It still fucked up my head. I can't control my reactions some-times, but it has nothing to do with you."

"Are you sure? I need you to be sure, Nina."

"I'm sure."

I hear steps approaching along with the faint clinking of plates and cutlery. It's a perfect excuse, so I lower my head and kiss him. It's meant to be just a quick kiss, but the moment I feel his lips on mine all rational thoughts go flying, and in the next moment my hands are clutching him to me with all my might. There is a need to somehow get closer to him ris-ing inside me, which seems silly since I'm already sprawled all over his chest with my legs on either side of him.

There is a gasp from somewhere behind me. I break the kiss and look over my shoulder to find the girl from yesterday standing in the doorway with a platter of food in her hands, her mouth half open and eyes wide. I yelp and quickly grab the hem of my lacy nightie that has ridden up my back and tug it down over Roman's hands which are currently clutching my butt. Hopefully, she'll skip retelling seeing my black lacy thong to everyone in the kitchen.

"Pakhan, I'm . . . sorry, I didn't know—"

"Just put it there and leave," Roman snaps from beneath me like he's mad at her for coming in, which doesn't make sense. We're doing all of this for her sake anyway. Well, he is at least. As for me, I'm not sure if I am pretending. And that scares the shit out of me.

I wait until the girl leaves, then look down at Roman. "I'll just . . . go now," I say, but I don't make a move to get off him.

He just stares at me with narrowed eyes, still holding his hands on my butt. The skin on his chest is so warm under my palms, his lips so very close. I would only have to lean forward a little to taste them again. Would it be so bad if I stayed here with him instead? Yeah, it probably would. I make a move to get down from him and his hands disappear from my backside immediately.

"I need to go buy some clothes," I say as I get down from the bed, grab a sandwich from the tray the maid left, and walk toward the door. "Your snobby wife wouldn't be caught dead walking around in one of my hoodies."

"I'll take you in the morning. Be ready at nine."

I look back at him and see him lying sprawled in the bed, his hands crossed behind his head, which makes his already huge frame look even larger. No one should be that good-looking. And I missed the opportunity to check out his tattoos, again. Damn.

"Okay. Good night then," I say and run out the room.

Chapter
six

 Roman

WHEN I GET INTO THE KITCHEN AT AROUND half past eight, Nina is already finishing her breakfast. Instead of joining her, I pour myself a glass of orange juice and drink it by the counter, because I'm not sure I'll be able to get up if I sit down now. Warren tormented me for almost two hours this morning in my physical therapy session, and I barely managed to shower and dress after it. I should have taken the wheelchair right away instead of crutches.

"We have to make a small detour before I take you shopping." I place my empty glass in the sink. "One of my men called about an issue I have to resolve. It won't take long."

"Is it okay if we drop by an art supply store, as well? Varya came in earlier to say my art supplies have arrived, but I need to buy more paints."

"Of course. I'll tell one of the guys to bring the boxes upstairs. Where do you want them?"

"In front of the window by the bookshelf. That's if you're

okay with me setting up my workspace there? I'll cover the floor and won't make a mess, I promise."

"Sure." I nod and turn to walk into my bedroom and get my wheelchair when a piercing pain slashes the whole length of my right leg. Fuck. I squeeze my eyes for a second, take a deep breath, and make a small step forward. I manage two more before I have to stop and take a short break.

"Roman?"

I look over my shoulder and find Nina watching me from her spot at the table. "Is everything okay?"

"Yes." I nod and continue dragging myself toward the bedroom, trying not to put too much weight on my right leg.

I grab the door handle and turn to Nina. "Stay in the car. I won't be long."

"Sure, honey." She smiles and cracks her lips. I shake my head and transfer myself from the car seat to the wheelchair Dimitri, my chief of security, is holding for me.

The warehouse is situated south of the city, on a lawn between two abandoned factories. The ground is rough, which makes it harder to push the wheels, but Dimitri knows damn well not to try and help me. We enter through a big door that's used for vehicles and stop in the middle of the huge hall where two of my men stand waiting.

"Who fucked up?" I bark as I enter, with Dimitri following after me.

"The driver," Mikhail answers. "He was pulled over by

a routine patrol for speeding. He was also drunk. The merchandise was confiscated."

"He was speeding while transporting my drugs. Drunk," I say, unbelieving. "Where is the idiot?"

"He managed to escape the cops. He's in the back room."

"Kill him," I say to Mikhail and turn to Anton. "Make sure the others are warned, so shit like this doesn't happen again."

"Yes, Pakhan."

"Show me the map. We'll need to change the route for the next few shipments."

It takes us around twenty minutes to set up the alternative route, and we spend almost an hour going over the shipments planned for the following two weeks and making necessary adjustments. Maybe I shouldn't have brought Nina, she's probably getting restless in the car while waiting this long.

When we finally get back to the car, Dimitri opens the door for me, and when I see Nina, I stop in mid-move. She is sitting cross-legged on the back seat, eyes closed. On the phone in her lap a video is playing, showing a woman in the same pose, muttering some new-age nonsense while Nina is speaking along. She looks ridiculous. "What are you doing?"

"Purging negative vibrations and channeling positive energy into my chakra points. Vova, here, said he didn't mind."

I turn my head to look at our driver. He's staring straight ahead, feigning composure, but I can see it on his face, he's barely managing not to burst out laughing.

"Do you want to try it, honey? It does wonders for re-leasing stress," Nina says, sounding completely serious, but I can see a twinkle of mischief in her eyes.

"We'll try something similar when we get home."

 Nina

There are three piles of clothes on the bench in the changing room. The biggest one has the things that don't fit and can't be altered. The middle one consists of clothes that are not the best fit—mostly jeans and two dresses—but which could be shortened. The boutique assistant took my measurements ear-lier, and promised to have them altered by their seamstress, and delivered in two days. These fancy boutiques certainly have outstanding customer service. I give the clothes that need to be shortened to the assistant who is waiting in front of the changing room and take the third and smallest pile with me to the cash register. I can't believe I managed to find something that fits.

Roman pays for my purchases with his card, then winds his arm around my waist and leans toward me. "I like that pink thong very much. You'll wear it for me tonight," he says and kisses me.

I know he's doing it only because his man, Dimitri, is in front of us collecting the bags, but I still feel the butterflies raging in my stomach. Dimitri doesn't comment, pretending nothing out of ordinary is happening, but I noticed the way his eyes widened when he saw us kiss. He's slightly older than

Roman—maybe late thirties—and handsome, with a few extra pounds around his middle.

Roman's hand comes to rest on my ass, and he squeezes it lightly.

"Stop ogling my chief of security, Nina," he says in my ear.

I cock an eyebrow and smile. "Sure, honey."

We head to the shoe store next to the boutique, and fifteen minutes later, I'm sitting on a chair with at least a dozen boxes scattered on the floor around me. When I see the prices on them, I almost faint and want to go to another store, but Roman doesn't want to hear it. So here I am, holding a pair of heels that cost a small fortune when I hear Roman approaching. He wheels himself so he's in front of me and leans in, takes the shoes from my hands, and places them in his lap.

"Left," he instructs and extends his hand.

I cross my legs and raise my left foot, placing my heel on his palm. He takes a shoe from his lap and, holding my leg around the ankle, slides it onto my foot.

"You have a foot fetish, Roman?"

"No. But it looks like I'm developing one," he says with his chin tucked and releases my leg. "Right."

He does the same with each pair, and by the time we're done, I'm seriously turned on. I had no idea my feet were an erogenous zone, or maybe it's the way he deliberately caresses the skin around my ankle every single time. I have a feeling every part of my body would become an erogenous zone if Roman touched it. Of course, I'll never allow things to come to that.

"We're taking them all," he says and motions for Dimitri who is standing by the entrance.

"Are you crazy?" I whisper, making sure Dimitri won't overhear. "We'll take only one pair."

"No."

"Roman!"

"All of them, Nina. Now, smile."

"Thank you, honey, I love them!" I beam at him and lean to place a quick kiss on his cheek.

"Dimitri will take you to the art supply shop and then to the car. Wait for me there. I need to drop by another store, and I'll be there shortly."

"Oh, that would be perfect. I'm not good at orienting myself in unfamiliar spaces."

"I know, love. Don't worry, it happens to everyone." He places a quick kiss on my lips and turns to leave the store, and I notice Dimitri watching him with confusion on his face.

"He's so sweet, isn't he?" I smile at Dimitri who just blinks at me. I quickly turn and walk out of the shop, so he won't hear me snorting.

CHAPTER
seven

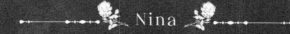 Nina

WHEN WE RETURN FROM OUR SHOPPING TRIP, the marriage official is already waiting for us in the living room of Roman's suite. The marriage license signing is highly anticlimactic. The guy says his thing, while Varya and Maxim act as our witnesses. A couple of yesses and four signatures later, Roman and I are husband and wife. I can't believe I got married in a pair of jeans I've owned since my freshman year of high school. It's one of the most bizarre things I've ever experienced. The rings are a nice touch, though. I don't know how Roman managed to find the wedding rings so fast. He probably went to a jewelry store while I was waiting with Vova and Dimitri in the car. I also got a second ring—a thick white gold band with a pale rock in the middle, which I suppose will pose as an engagement ring. It's probably fake, because the real deal would cost a fortune. I like it anyway.

After they leave, Roman takes his laptop, says he has work

to do, and locks himself in his room. He doesn't even come out to eat the lunch Varya brings.

I put my new clothes into the wardrobe, and finish one painting before my inspiration dries up. Now, I'm getting royally bored. Maybe I should order some items and start redecorating the house as planned. Maybe some lamps. I sprawl onto the sofa and close my eyes.

"Lamps. I love lamps. The bigger the better. Gold, with big black lampshades. And tresses," I mumble to myself. "They'll bring in the sophisticated look, so I'll put them everywhere. The staff are going to hate those things. They're hell to dust and—"

"No lamps." I hear Roman's deep voice coming directly from above me, but I just smile and continue, keeping my eyes closed.

"And my husband hates my lamps. But he knows he has zero interior design knowledge, and because he's so crazy about me, he decides to leave my lamps in peace. All fourteen of them."

I open my eyes and find Roman bending over me, his eyes narrowed. He's in his wheelchair again. Strange. He usually uses crutches when he's in his suite.

"Decided to finally get out of your cave, I see." I cock an eyebrow.

"You should get dressed. We're going down for dinner in thirty minutes."

"Slutty, serious, or something in the middle?"

"Middle will work."

"Damn, I wish you picked slutty."

 Roman

My fucking knee has been acting up again. It happens every once in a while. I took some painkillers this afternoon and spent the rest of the day working from my bed, hoping it would help. It did, but just barely. I hate this chair, but the thing that bothers me more than the chair itself is Nina seeing me in it. She's nothing to me. We have a limited-time deal, and then she'll be gone. Still, it bothers me.

The door to her room opens, and when Nina comes out, the room starts pulsating with energy. She's wearing tight black jeans and a yellow silky blouse, paired with heels in the same color. Her hair is pulled into a high ponytail that falls down her back. Nina normally doesn't wear makeup, and I like that. She doesn't need any. But tonight, she must have decided that this is a special occasion, because her lips are a deep red, and she did something with her eyes to accentuate their shape and color. Funny thing, I miss her nose ring.

"Ready?" I ask.

"As much as I'll ever be. Lead the way, husband."

When we enter the big dining room on the first floor, everybody is already seated and chatting. The moment they notice us, the chatter dies, and they all stand up. The tension is so thick, you can cut through it with a knife, so I decide to get to the point right away.

"This is my wife, Nina Petrova," I declare.

Everybody stares at me, and then their gazes move to Nina.

"Hi!" She smiles and waves.

Nobody comments. Good.

"We had a municipal wedding this afternoon but decided to delay the church wedding till summer. Nina wants to have an outdoor ceremony."

"Yes. It will be by the lake." She kisses me on the cheek. "Thank you for humoring me, honey."

"I know this is a bit sudden, but it doesn't change things. If anyone dares to disrespect my wife, they will not like the consequences." I make sure to pin every man sitting at the table with my gaze until I come to my uncle. "Doesn't matter who they are. Is that clear?"

"Yes, Pakhan," everybody says in unison.

"Nina, you already know Maxim and Dimitri," I say, and they nod. I turn my gaze to the other side of the table next.

"This is Leonid, my uncle."

I watch for his reaction, but Leonid is far from stupid. He nods, his face a perfect mask of politeness, but there is no missing the evil glint in his eyes.

"On Leonid's left is Mikhail, the brothers Ivan and Kostya, and Sergei. On Dimitri's right are Yuri, Pavel, and Anton. These are my closest men, and I trust them with my life. And from now on, with yours as well."

Nina turns toward the men at the table. All of them fist their right hand, hit their chest in unison, and nod while she watches them with wide eyes. Her face is controlled, but from her stance and the way she's squeezing my forearm, I know she's in a bit of a shock. As it appears, my little flower didn't understand exactly what she's gotten herself into before tonight.

"Let's eat," I say and nod to Varya who is waiting by the door. She motions with her hand to Olga, Valentina, and Galina to bring the food.

The dinner passes as I expect, mostly in silence. Every few minutes someone throws a quick look in Nina's direction, which I'm sure she notices but pretends not to. And Nina is very good at pretending—almost disturbingly good. I was expecting her to overdo it, act out too much, giggle. There's none of that. She leans closer between bites to ask something and touches my hand every now and then. Everything seems so genuine that even I, knowing it's all for show, find it hard not to believe in her act.

"I changed my mind," she whispers in my ear and breaks my train of thought. "We'll keep this table. It's monumental."

"I'm glad you feel that way."

"But the drapes will have to go, honey. That shade of brown is so depressing. My feng shui guru says we should always throw out the things that depress us."

The sound of her voice is completely serious, her face a picture of perfect sincerity, but her eyes are laughing at me. I lean toward her.

"Then we'll burn them," I say and kiss her.

CHAPTER eight

Nina

SOMETHING IS NOT RIGHT. I REMEMBER ROMAN mentioning an important meeting planned for this morning. It's after nine, and he still hasn't come out of his room. I heard his phone ring around eight, and then him speaking to someone. Fifteen minutes later Valentina brought us breakfast, saying that Roman instructed her to leave it with me.

Maybe I should check on him. I put away the paintbrush on the small plate I keep near my canvas, wipe my hands, and turn toward Roman's room. Suddenly, his door opens, and he wheels himself out and toward the kitchen. He's wearing only sweatpants, his upper body fully on display, and I can't stop staring.

Roman doesn't even notice me approaching. Instead, he goes to the set of drawers near the sink and starts rummaging through the top one. When he doesn't find what he's looking for, he mumbles something in Russian, shuts the drawer with a bang, and moves to the next one.

"Need any help there?"

"Nope," he snaps.

I watch him fish out a white bottle from the drawer, take out two pills from it and swallow them. He looks at the bottle again, takes out another pill, and throws the bottle back into the drawer. While he's grabbing a bottle of water from the fridge, I take the opportunity to have a look at the label to see what he took. It's painkillers. Finally, he turns his chair to face me, and I gasp.

"You look like hell." His face is pale and his eyes bloodshot. "Did you get any sleep at all?"

"Not really."

I follow him to his room and watch as he enters the walk-in wardrobe and comes back with a pair of pants and a shirt on his lap.

"What are you doing?"

"I have a meeting in twenty minutes. Please leave, I have to change."

"You're in no state to go anywhere, Roman."

He ignores me, puts his clothes on the bed next to him, and starts to stand up from the wheelchair, but the moment he tries to straighten, a hiss escapes his mouth, and he drops back down. "Fuck it!"

"Well, I guess this means there won't be any disrobing involved in the near future," I say. "Come on, let's get you into bed."

"Bed won't work. My knee is stiff, I can't straighten my leg."

"How about the sofa? We could put something under your leg and watch a movie."

Roman looks at me like I'm insane. "I can't spend the day watching movies. I have a criminal empire to run."

"Yeah, you won't be running anywhere today, literally or figuratively. You just took a triple dose of painkillers, so you'll probably be out in less than an hour, sleeping like a baby."

"Shit," he curses, then grumbles something in Russian and shakes his head.

"I have no idea what you just said, but I agree." I nod. "Do you need to call them to cancel?"

"Yeah. Give me the phone."

When we get to the living room, Roman somehow manages to transfer himself to the sofa. I grab one of the big pillows to put under his leg, then go to his room and bring back a blanket, which I throw over him. Roman follows my every move but doesn't comment. I don't think he's accustomed to having someone fuss over him. I might be wrong, but I believe he secretly enjoys it. I head to the kitchen and check out the breakfast left on the tray. It's some kind of handmade pie with fruit filling. I take a bite. Still warm— it'll do.

"I started watching a movie last night, do you want to join me? I've only watched fifteen minutes or so. I'll bring you up to speed," I shout while I'm taking a carafe of orange juice from the fridge.

"Sounds good."

"Any chance there's popcorn somewhere?" I ask as I open the cupboard.

"I doubt it."

"What about the kitchen downstairs? We can't watch a movie without popcorn."

"I have no idea. Call Varya and ask her."

I carry over the tray with breakfast and place it on the low table in front of the sofa, then turn to Roman. "You take an awful lot of space. Head up, please."

"And you're bossy today," he says but rises onto his elbows.

I sit down in the spot where his head had been, prop my legs onto the table and tap on my thigh. Roman slowly lowers himself back down, putting his head on my lap. He hands me his phone with Varya's number already selected.

 Roman

I just can't wait to hear this.

"Varya, I'm sorry if I interrupted you," Nina chirrups into the phone. "Do you maybe have popcorn somewhere?"

I don't hear the reply, but I can imagine Varya's face. I'm pretty sure no one's ever seen popcorn in this house. We have bombs, a few crates of grenades, and a ton of ammunition in the garage. But no popcorn.

"Yes, popcorn . . . Well, to eat. We're watching a movie." She listens to Varya's response. "What do you mean 'who's we'? Me and Roman." Another pause, and then, "Yes, Varya, I am serious . . . No, that's not necessary, . . . I . . . Okay, thank you."

She places the phone on the table, looks down at me, and makes a disgusted face. "There's no popcorn, but she'll bring us peanuts. I hate those, but she's eager to come over."

Of course, she is.

The knock on the door comes less than five minutes later. Varya opens the door and walks toward the living room but stops midway to stare at us. Her eyes glide over me lying on the sofa under the blanket, and when they come to my head resting on Nina's lap, her eyebrows hit her hairline. Then she approaches, leaves a bowl of peanuts on the table, and throws another look at me, her eyes going to Nina's hand which is buried in my hair, her fingers playing with one of the strands.

"I could have come down for that," Nina says.

"Nonsense, child. Do you two need anything else?"

"Can we get the lunch here, later I mean? I don't think Roman will be leaving this couch anytime soon."

Varya throws me a look and smirks. "Oh, I'm sure he won't."

When Varya leaves, Nina leans back and starts the movie. She's bringing me up to speed on what's happened so far, but I don't really pay attention to what she's saying, and instead close my eyes and enjoy the feel of her hand running through my hair. The painkillers start to kick in, and I could probably get up and go back to my room or at least sit up, but instead, I stay in the same position and listen to Nina's voice describing in great detail how the murder in the movie happened and drift away.

"I'm not bringing you the crutches, Roman."

I stare at Nina from my sitting position on the sofa and grind my teeth. We spent the whole morning and a good part of the afternoon lounging in the living room. I even managed to sleep for almost two hours, and my knee is much better.

"Nina!"

"Roman."

"Get me the fucking crutches. Please."

"No crutches for you today," she says and pushes the wheelchair toward me.

"You are overstepping your boundaries," I bite out.

"Sue me."

I curse, get into the fucking chair, and wheel myself into my bedroom. After I take a shower and change, I take my laptop and go back to the living room. I hate to admit it, but there's still some piercing pain in my knee. It's not that bad, but it's still easier to be sitting; and, since I'm in the chair anyway, I decide to do some work.

"I'm going to the office," I say and nod toward the door. "Let's go, I'll give you the tour along the way."

She follows me down the east corridor, and I point to each door we pass. "The second office, which I don't use. Two guest bedrooms, locked. The gym. I work out there every morning, and three times a week I have a physical therapist."

"Why do you keep the guest rooms locked? What do you do when you have people staying over?"

"I don't invite people to stay over in my house. It's a security risk."

We come to a stop at the top of the stairway, and I nod toward the hallway that extends into the west wing. "My men have rooms there. It will be hard to bug any of those without someone becoming suspicious."

The elevator takes us to the ground floor, and I turn right toward the "business" part of the house.

"The lounge." I motion toward widely opened double doors, showing a large living space used by my men. "On the right, Leonid's office."

"What does he do?"

"Leonid is officially in charge of the finances, but in reality, Kostya and Ivan do all the work. Mikhail handles distribution and some other stuff. He has his offices at home and in one of the warehouses, so he's rarely here."

"Mikhail is the big guy with the eye patch?"

I stop for a moment, take Nina's forearm, and turn her toward me. "What happened to Mikhail is personal, please don't ask around about it."

"Okay."

"One other thing. When Mikhail is around, try not to touch him by accident. He . . . doesn't deal well with skin-to-skin contact."

Nina's eyes widen, but she doesn't ask anything further, just nods.

"Good. This door here leads to the basement. You won't go down there under any circumstances," I say.

"Why?"

Telling her that's where we usually torture people is out of the question. "You just don't."

"Did you already . . . you know?" She points to her ear.

"Maxim handled that already."

"What's his position?"

"He's my second-in-command. Dimitri works with him, but he mainly handles the security."

"And the rest?"

"Pavel is in charge of club business. Anton and Yuri handle the foot soldiers. Sergei, the tall blond guy, handles negotiations as well as all our legitimate deals, like real estate and rentals. He rarely comes here, but when he does, try to avoid him. He's got issues."

"Everybody has issues, Roman."

"Not like Sergei's. Believe me. Stay away from him."

"And all of them live here?"

"All of the men you met last night have rooms upstairs, but only Leonid, Pavel, Kostya, and Ivan live here."

"And what about the staff? Maids?"

"Valentina and Olga also have rooms on the east side, where the kitchen is. Varya also has a small apartment there. The rest go home every evening."

"Is Varya your housekeeper?"

"She was the housekeeper for the old pakhan. When I took over, I set her up for life, so she wouldn't need to work anymore. She didn't want to leave. Still doesn't. So, I let her run the house; it makes her happy."

"She doesn't want to leave you, you mean."

"Yes."

I see it in her eyes, she wants to ask more but she doesn't, and I don't volunteer. Some things are better left unsaid.

"This is Maxim's office, then Dimitri's." I point to the doors on the right. "Kostya and Ivan share an office, it's the door next to Leonid's. Mine is the last one down the hallway. If I'm not upstairs, I'm probably here. I'll give you Maxim's and Dimitri's numbers later, just in case."

"Can we see the kitchen?"

"If you insist."

"You sound reluctant. Is something wrong with the kitchen?"

Everything is wrong with the damn kitchen. "You'll see."

Nina

We're right in front of the open kitchen doors when something big and metallic falls to the floor with a crash. There is a split second of utter silence followed by throaty yelling so loud I flinch. When we get inside, I look around and feel like I just walked into a madhouse.

A huge bearded man in his sixties, wearing a white chef's apron and a bandanna over his head, is standing with his hands on his hips and shouting what I assume are Russian obscenities. He's not very tall, but he's as wide as a truck. A big, overturned pot of what looks like soup lays on the floor near his feet. Valentina and two other women, who I presume are Olga and Galina, run around the kitchen, getting rags and then kneel to wipe the floor. Meanwhile, the cook stands still in the middle of a big puddle of soup. Varya is at the other end of the kitchen, near the big fridge, pointing at the cook and also shouting in Russian.

On the far right, there is a small dining table where Kostya and Dimitri are sitting; they're drinking coffee and discussing something. They don't look even slightly perturbed by the yelling match happening behind them.

Nobody even notices us.

"Is it always like this in here?" I mumble.

"Most of the time."

The two women wiping the floor start arguing. One of them throws the rag to the other and walks toward the sink.

"They are just under your suite. How come I've never heard them before," I ask in awe.

"I got the kitchen soundproofed."

"Good call." I nod, still staring at the chaos with amazement. "Should we leave them to it?"

Roman looks around himself, reaches for a thick cutting board, and smashes it down onto the metal counter beside him. The sound reverberates across the room, making me jump. Everyone shuts up.

"This is Nina," Roman says. "My wife."

I smile widely and wave in their general direction.

"Nina Petrova!" they all shout and nod at the same time.

"Oh, you can just call me Nina."

"No, they can't!" Roman barks.

"Honey!"

"End of discussion."

"You are so stern, Roman." I pout just a little, then turn toward the kitchen staff. "He is, isn't he?"

They all watch me like I'm a simpleton. Perfect. I turn to Roman. "Can I stay here?"

"You sure about that?"

"Yup."

"All right. I'll be in my office."

"I'll drop by later." I place a quick kiss on his cheek.

Ten minutes later, I am sitting at the table in the corner, trying to discuss the breakfast with Igor, the cook. He only speaks Russian, so Varya is acting as my translator. It's not going well.

"Igor thinks you didn't like his piroshki this morning," Varya says. "He is afraid that the pakhan will fire him or worse, if he hears you don't like his food."

Oh, for crying out loud. I have this urge to start banging my forehead on the tabletop. Instead, I smile sweetly. "I loved the pie. It was delicious, and I'll make sure Roman knows. I'd even love to learn how to make it. Just, can I please get some cereal for breakfast as well?"

Varya translates for me, and Igor beams. He jumps from his chair babbling something and motioning with his hand. I follow him toward the kitchen island where he puts an apron over my head and starts taking out some ingredients from the cupboard. I turn to look over my shoulder at Varya, hoping she'll tell me what's going on, but she just laughs and shakes her head.

Roman

I finish going over the numbers with Leonid and Kostya, and look at my watch. It's almost seven in the evening; the whole afternoon flew by with all the meetings and paperwork that I was behind with. I wonder what Nina is doing. She said she would drop by but didn't, and I'll be damned if I know why, but it doesn't sit well with me.

"How long do you plan on continuing with this thing, Roman?"

I look at Leonid who is sitting in a chair on the other side of my desk. Kostya's already left, so it's only the two of us. "What thing?"

"The marriage. You didn't even have a church wedding. People will talk."

"No, they won't."

"How do you know?"

"Because I will silence them, Leonid. The same way I silenced my father." I cock my head to the side. "Do you remember that night?"

He tenses and doesn't say anything, but I notice the vein pulsing in his neck. Yes, he remembers that night very well.

"If you don't have any other questions, you can leave." I nod toward the door.

He gets up and marches out of my office.

Leonid has started acting strangely the last couple of months. He's always been a lazy piece of shit who prefers to have other people work for him while he takes all the credit. He's been trying to take over more responsibilities from Kostya recently, which is the main reason I suspect he had something to do with that bomb. I'll have to do something about him—proof or no proof—and soon. Now, however, I'm dying to know what my peculiar little wife has been doing the whole afternoon, so I call Varya.

"Where is she?"

"Still here in the kitchen," Varya says, her tone amused.

"What has she been doing there this whole time?"

"Come and see for yourself."

I wheel myself down the long hallway and into the kitchen. Nina is standing by the work surface, placing round pieces of dough into a big pan while Igor is standing behind her, overseeing. Even though she's wearing an apron, her pink lacy blouse and jeans are covered in flour. Her ponytail is askew, and she has something that looks like jam on her left cheek.

"Igor is teaching her how to make piroshki," Varya says as she comes to stand by me. "They're on their third batch."

"Igor speaks only Russian. How can he teach her anything?"

"I have no idea. He tells her what to do, and when she does it wrong, he yells."

My head snaps to the side to look at Varya. "He yelled at my wife?"

"She yelled at him more."

"What for?"

"Well, he yelled because she burned the first batch. She yelled because he didn't say how long they should stay in the oven. Neither of them knew what the other was yelling about. It was hilarious."

We stand at the door and watch them.

"What happened with the second batch?" I ask. "Burned as well?"

"The second one was good. They just took it out of the oven when boys started coming in for lunch. Everyone who passed took one or two, and in five minutes, they were all gone." She laughs. "Oh, she was so mad."

"Why? Did she want to eat them all by herself?"

Varya turns to me, and there is a mischievous and satisfied

look in her eyes, like a cat who got the cream. "No, Roman. She was mad because they didn't leave any for you."

At that moment Nina raises her head, our gazes connect, and she smiles at me. It's like the sun has suddenly broken through the dark clouds, hitting me with its warmth, and I find myself wishing this was real and not just an act. Her heels click on the floor as she is approaches, echoing in the big space.

"They ate your piroshki," she says and puts her hands on her hips.

She is so bloody cute when she's mad. I lean forward and grab her around her waist with one arm, and under her knees with the other. Lifting her, I deposit her onto my lap.

She squeaks and wraps her arms around my neck. "I've got flour all over your shirt."

"I don't care," I say and grab the wheels. "Hold tight."

Her eyes widen, but she tightens her arms around my neck.

"Open the door for us, Varya," I call over my shoulder, turn the chair around and wheel us into the hallway.

With Nina's legs dangling over the side of the chair, it requires a little more maneuvering to handle the right wheel, but I manage, and take us across the hallway and into the elevator. She's laughing like crazy along the way, with her face buried into my neck, and it feels so damn good.

My light mood evaporates the moment we exit the elevator and I see Leonid standing at the top of the stairs, looking at us with a calculated stare. I ignore him and take us to the door of my suite.

"Thanks for the ride." Nina giggles and stands to open the door.

"Any time, malysh." Inside, I shut the door behind me. "Come, we need to talk."

"Is something wrong?"

"Maybe. Go get changed, I'll be waiting in the kitchen."

Nina

When I enter the kitchen, freshly showered and wearing clean clothes, I find Roman rummaging through the fridge. He's changed as well, into a pair of jeans and a white T-shirt that stretches tightly over his wide back. I can't help but stare.

"How's the knee?" I ask when I manage to stop ogling him. He's on his crutches again, so I suppose he's feeling better.

"Back to normal," he says and closes the fridge. "Or as normal as it was a few days ago. I have to call to schedule my therapist for tomorrow. I had to cancel today's session."

I walk over and stand next to him, sure that I've finally overcome my body's idiotic response to his size. My arm brushes his elbow accidentally, and I flinch.

"Sorry," I whisper and close my eyes, angry with myself. I hate this.

I feel Roman's arm around my waist, and in the next moment, I find myself sitting on the counter.

"You don't have to do that all the time," I sigh.

"I don't mind."

"It's absurd. Did it hurt your leg?"

"I'm sorry to tell you, but you are kind of small, Nina. My leg is perfectly fine."

"Everyone is kind of small around you, Roman." I roll my eyes and swat his shoulder. "Does the physical therapy help?"

"Yes, but it's slow. It took me two months to walk on crutches. One more to use them without any significant pain. Warren says we'll try the cane in a couple of weeks, see how it goes." He moves to the counter beside where I'm sitting, reaching for a glass and the carafe of orange juice.

"And after that?"

He doesn't reply right away, seeming to concentrate on pouring the orange juice.

"My knee is too fucked up. The cane is probably the best I can do."

By the way he avoids looking me in the eyes, I can guess he doesn't like that outcome.

"You'll be sexy with the cane, Roman. Very aristocratic looking."

His eyes snap up to mine and his lips lift in a smile. "And I'm not sexy now?"

Oh, you have no idea how much, I want to say. Instead, I just laugh. "Are you fishing for compliments, Pakhan? My God, you are so vain." I nudge him playfully, and we both chuckle. When the laughter trails off, I change the subject. "You said you have something to discuss."

"Yes. I need you to bug Leonid's room first. His office as well, but his room is the priority."

"Okay. How do we go about getting me into his room? I could sneak in while he's working."

"There's always somebody around, a maid or some of the guys." Roman shifts his weight away from his bad leg and leans his hip on the counter. "I'll have to think about it."

"What if I mess up?"

"You won't." He reaches for me with his hand as if he is going to touch my face, but then reconsiders and turns away. "Did you inform your parents that we got married?"

I cringe. "Not yet. Do I have to?"

"Yes."

"Shit. Mom is going to kill me. She's always talked about how she wanted to organize a huge wedding if I ever found someone crazy enough to marry me. Maybe I'll just message her."

A muscle ticks in Roman's jaw, and he leans toward me until our noses almost touch. "You can't inform your mother that you got married via text message, Nina. You'll call her and ask her and your father to come over for dinner."

"Here?" I blink at him. "I can't ask them to come here. When my mom sees all the guys with guns, she'll think I married into mafia!"

Roman's eyebrows almost reach his hairline. "And your mother would be right."

"Yeah, but can we leave out that small detail? She freaked out when she saw my nose piercing. My mother is extremely conservative; she even irons her towels. I'm not sure how she'll react to the fact I married a crime lord."

He laughs and shakes his head. "We'll take them to a restaurant."

Roman

I am not a fan of Nina's mother.

As expected, she's shocked when Nina tells her we

got married so suddenly, and to a man they've never met. However, based on the looks she's been tossing in my direction throughout dinner, she is more concerned that I'm using a wheelchair than the fact her daughter married a stranger.

"Are you pregnant, Nina?" she asks casually between two bites of cake.

Next to me, Nina chokes on her wine.

"Jesus, Mom," she says when she manages to recover. "Of course not. We met a week ago."

"But we're working on it," I throw in and take Nina's hand. "Aren't we, love?"

Nina blinks at me, then smiles and leans in to kiss me. "We sure are."

Nina's father is sitting on the other side of the table, barely speaking. He's been avoiding my gaze the whole time. When he does look at me, he quickly looks away and hides his trembling hands under the table. I don't like Samuel Grey, either, and it has nothing to do with the fact that he stole my money. He knows very well who I am, and he still let his daughter marry me to save his own ass. What a pitiful excuse for a human being.

On the table, my phone rings, showing Pavel's name. It's six in the evening, and the clubs are not open yet, so it can't be club business. I take the call.

"Pakhan. We have a problem."

Of course, we do. "I'm listening."

"Ukrainians are here. Shevchenko wants to renegotiate the terms."

"Tell him to contact Sergei. He's in charge of that."

"They already met earlier today, and Shevchenko says he has no intention of negotiating with him ever again." There is a silent pause on the other side of the line, then, "Sergei tried to cut off his hand."

"Wonderful." I squeeze the bridge of my nose and sigh. "Where are you? At Ural?"

"Yes."

"I'll be there in twenty minutes."

I put the phone in my pocket and turn to Nina. "I have to go. Dimitri will stay and take you back when you're done."

"Is everything okay?" she asks.

"Yes." I nod and kiss her, then seeing the way her mother is watching us, I add, "Put on something sexy and wait for me. I won't be long."

Nina

My eyes follow Roman as he wheels himself to the exit where Dimitri is standing by the wall. They speak quietly and Roman leaves. Did something happen? It sounded serious.

"Are you sure you did the right thing, Nina?" my mother asks.

I turn to face her. "What do you mean?"

"Marrying this man, after just two days." She looks at me with a mix of exasperation and annoyance. "I mean, I shouldn't be surprised, you always did things your way, but still."

I roll my eyes. "This man has a name. And we're crazy about each other. Why wait?"

"I understand why you fell for him. He's older, rich, sophisticated. Extremely handsome."

"There you go." I smile and lean back in my chair. "Your dream finally came true. I thought you would be thrilled."

"He's in a wheelchair, Nina."

"Zara!" my father whisper-yells from the other side of the table, and glances at Dimitri standing by the door. "Shut up."

"Don't silence me, Samuel. I want the best for my child, and I have the right to be concerned."

"Keep your concerns to yourself, Mom," I snap.

She leans forward over the table. "What happened to him? A car accident?"

"Yes." I toss my napkin on the plate. "He got a serious injury to his leg a few months ago. Does that satisfy your curiosity?"

She grinds her teeth and watches me through narrowed eyes. "Can he walk?"

I stare at my mother. "I just told you. I married him because I'm in love with him. Why would that matter?" I find it concerning how fast and easily those words came out of my mouth.

"Why?" She widens her eyes at me and turns to my father. "Why aren't you saying anything? Did you know about this, Samuel?"

"Zara, for God's sake, just shut up!"

She ignores my father completely. "Is this some kind of rebellion, Nina? Another one of your phases?"

That's it. I've had enough. I grab my phone from the table, stand up, and head toward the exit, leaving my parents sitting at the table.

CHAPTER
nine

 Nina

I COCK MY HEAD TO THE SIDE AND REGARD THE BIG canvas in front of me. Too bright. Grabbing the palette, I use the brush to mix some more black with the pale gray, and then start adding sharper shadows.

Four pieces are done and waiting to be sent to the gallery. Ten, when combined with the six I sent before my life took such a drastic turn. I have five more to finish by the end of next week to make my deadline for the exhibition. They would have to wait, though, because I've decided to work on the big guy next. Usually, I finalize all the standard pieces first and work on the main piece last. Not this time. Looks like Roman not only managed to mess up my head but also my creative process.

I haven't seen him much in the last two weeks—usually only in the mornings, before he goes downstairs to his office to do whatever mafia crime lords do, and in the evenings when he returns for dinner. I make sure to drop by his office at least twice a day, always at the most inconvenient times.

Often, there's been someone else inside with him. On my way there and back, I wander around the house, rearranging potted plants and paintings or doing similar idiotic stuff. Other than that, I spend most of my time in the suite, which has left me with a lot of time to paint.

Yesterday, Maxim came by to give me a quick newbie-friendly course on planting the bugs. I expected it to involve wires and sneaking around with a screwdriver, unscrewing vents, and placing small microphones inside. Instead, he gave me a few black plastic things that looked like phone chargers, only without the cables. All I had to do was get into a room and plug it into a socket not in plain sight. Scary. The moment he'd left, I walked through the whole suite twice, checking every socket.

Today, I'm still fighting a lingering urge to look at every outlet I pass.

Lowering the brush, I take a few steps back and regard my big baby with a huge grin on my face. Yup, that's perfect. Carefully, I turn the painting so it faces the wall instead of the door, in case Roman comes in. He never comes into my room, but it doesn't hurt to be extra careful. I don't want him to see the big guy before the exhibition, which is why I decided to work on it in my room instead of beside the big bookshelf where I work on my other pieces.

I check the clock on the nightstand, then look at my reflection in the mirror. I'm covered in black and red paint up to my elbows, and I have several gray and red splotches all over my shirt. Some on my face too. My delivery will be here shortly, I should probably change and wash my face and hands before going downstairs to wait for them.

Roman

I'm on the phone with Mikhail, who's giving me the report for the last shipment, when there's a knock on the door and Dimitri enters the office.

"I'll call you back," I tell Mikhail and end the call.

"Some things have arrived for Nina Petrova," Dimitri says and looks at me pointedly.

"So? Tell some of the men to take them to the east wing."

"What should we do with the lamps?"

"What lamps?" I ask, and then I remember.

Shit. I put my elbows onto the desk and press the heels of my hands into my eyes. "Big? Gold with black?"

"Yes."

"How many?"

"Fourteen," he deadpans.

"Fourteen lamps . . ." I sigh. "Put them into the library for now."

"Alright. What about the animal?" he asks, and my head snaps up.

"What . . . animal?"

"Small. Black. It's in a carrier so I'm not sure what it is. Looks like a dog, but it sounds strange."

I grab the phone and call Nina. "Did you seriously order an animal online?"

"Excuse me?"

"Dimitri says there's a dog that came with your decoration stuff."

"Oh, that's Brando. I'm coming right down."

I stare at the phone in my hand. Brando. I'm going to kill her.

At the front door, I park my wheelchair at the top of the stairs and regard a bunch of boxes in different sizes covering half of the driveway. On the side, fourteen transparent rectangular boxes are lined up in a row, each with a wide gold ribbon tied around it. All of them hold the same lamp, the ugliest things I've ever set my eyes on.

Nina runs out of the house, dashes down the steps, and stops at the dog carrier that's been placed on one of the boxes. She opens the carrier, takes out a scrawny dog the size of a small cat and starts cooing to him.

"What's that?" Dimitri asks.

"A Chihuahua."

We watch Nina rummage through a few boxes, keeping the dog in the crook of her left arm. She takes out a leash from one of the boxes, clasps it to the collar, and sets the dog down. It starts running around her legs, letting out strange hamster-like barks.

"Let Varya know about the dog. She'll be very . . . excited. Send someone to buy some dog food," I say and turn to walk back to my office.

 Nina

I spend an hour walking Brando through the house and garden, so he can get the feel of the space. He's a bit jumpy because of all the new people, but he finally settles down into his bed in the corner of my room and goes to sleep.

Passing the kitchen, I grab an apple from the bowl and head to my workspace by the library. There are still several more hours left of natural light, and I plan on using them to work on the remaining five pieces for my exhibition. I should probably call my manager to tell him to send the courier for the finished paintings. Mark likes having as many of them as possible a few days before the event so he can organize the photographer and catalog printing.

I pull out my phone from the back pocket of my jeans and give Mark a call while I rearrange the finalized pieces along the big window.

When he answers, I chirp into the phone, "Hey, love."

"I know that tone," he groans. "You're behind schedule again."

"Of course not. I would never do that to you."

"Damn it, Nina. How behind are you?"

"A few days. But the big guy is done. I have five left. Can you send someone for the others? I'll send you the address."

"You've moved?"

"Yup. Long story."

"Will you be able to finish on time?"

"I'll try my best, babe."

There's some grumbling and a sigh. "Send me a photo of the big guy."

"I'm not sending you a photo, you'll have to wait and see for yourself, Mark. Bye." I put the phone back in my pocket and reach for one of the blank canvases.

"Who the fuck is Mark?"

I jump and spin around to find Roman glaring down at me.

"Why do you call him babe?" he demands. "And what kind of photo are you sending him?"

I blink at him and take a bite of my apple. "My pimp. All of us girls call him babe. And I'm sending a photo of my boobs."

He narrows his eyes on me but doesn't say anything.

"Oh, for God's sake, Roman. Mark is my manager and the owner of the gallery where I'm having my exhibition. He wanted photos of the paintings."

"Why do you call him babe?"

"Everybody calls him babe. Including his husband."

Roman's stance visibly relaxes, and his eyes lose their murderous gleam. Is he jealous?

"Can I see the paintings?" he asks.

So, it looks like we're just going to ignore his strange behavior. Works for me, because I don't want to dwell on the fact that I like the idea of him being jealous.

"Yes," I reply. "Just don't touch, some aren't dry yet."

Roman approaches the canvases and regards each one for a few moments until he stops in front of the newest one. "Is that . . . Igor?" He points the tip of the crutch toward the painting.

"Yes."

"Why does he have a megaphone instead of his head? And is that . . . a dead chicken under his arm?"

"You are extremely perceptive, Pakhan."

He looks at me over his shoulder and smirks. "And where's my painting? You promised me your self-portrait."

"Naked one. I remember. It'll have to wait; I need to finish the remaining exhibition pieces. Or I could do my self-portrait as one of those, I'm sure the critics will love it." I shrug. "We might need to add an "eighteen plus" label on the—"

"No."

"Then you'll have to wait."

"I'll wait." He turns and looks me over. "Are you hungry?"

His change of subject catches me unprepared. "A little."

"Let's go out for lunch."

Roman

I take Nina to a posh restaurant downtown, and we spend almost two hours there. She describes what she has planned for the exhibition, and I let her talk while watching her—her smiling eyes, the way she waves her hands in front of her face when she's excited, or how she leans forward, whispering in a low voice when she gossips about her colleagues who share the gallery. She must be aware that no one could hear her— the place is only half full, and none of the tables close to us are taken. Still, she keeps her tiny hand over her mouth, chatting about walking in on one of the other artists as she was grop-ing the guy from finance behind the gallery door.

There have been a lot of women in my life, but with Nina in front of me, they all just fade away. We've never even kissed properly, other than for the sake of the show, but I don't re-member ever being this drawn to someone. It's like she's be-witched me.

"What's the deal with the dog?"

"I borrowed him from my aunt." She grins and takes a sip of her wine.

"You borrowed a dog?" I stare at her.

"Technically, I offered to watch him for a few weeks. That should be enough time for him to do his part."

"And that would be?"

"Well, you know how dogs are always running around the house, getting into rooms, and hiding? Brando loves that, so I guess I'll be chasing him around the house quite a lot in the following days. Who knows where he'll end up?" She grins at me. "Maybe even in Leonid's room at some point."

I laugh and shake my head at her idea. "You are a dangerous woman, malysh."

"What does that mean?"

"Malysh? It's an term of endearment. It means little one."

She tilts her head to the side and the corners of her lips curl upward in a small smirk. "Well, as I already said, most people are little compared to you, Roman."

The waiter comes to fill our drinks. When Nina takes her glass, I notice her wedding ring is rather loose, so I reach out, take her hand in mine, and inspect the ring. "We should get this resized."

"Don't bother. The engagement ring is keeping it in place. It's durable by the way. I spilled some paint over my hand the other day and had to scrub it. It didn't even get scratched."

"It's rather hard to scratch a diamond."

Nina looks at me, blinks, then looks down at the ring like it's going to bite her. "This thing is real?"

"Of course, it's real."

"Shit!" She flattens her hand and stares disbelievingly at the two-carat princess-cut diamond. Her mouth opens and closes without words. Then she covers the ring protectively with her other hand and leans toward me. "Can I swap it with one that has glass instead?"

"No."

"Please?"

"You are not wearing a glass ring. End of discussion."

She scrunches her nose and mumbles something that sounds like "add devil's horns," but I probably misheard because it doesn't make any sense.

"Let's go home," I say and reluctantly let go of her hand. "We can watch a movie."

"Don't you have work to do?"

"I'm done for today. You?"

"My pimp is going to kill me. I'm already behind, but a movie sounds nice."

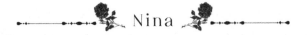

Nina

After we get back, I take a quick shower, change into leggings and an oversized T-shirt, and head to the kitchen to prepare popcorn. Roman apparently loves orange juice, he drinks liters of it, so I squeeze a few oranges for him and take it to the living room.

He's already there, sitting with his arms over the back of the sofa, his right leg stretched out in front of him with the heel propped on the table.

"You look strange in casual clothes." I place the bowl and the juice on the table, and nod toward his sweats and T-shirt.

"Oh? How so?"

"I don't know. Less pakhanish, I guess." I shrug and drop down on the sofa next to him "What are we watching?"

"I don't care. Move over."

I move to the corner, and Roman lies down on the sofa, places his head in my lap, and closes his eyes.

"Does your leg hurt?"

"Yes," he says, but there is a slight delay in his reply.

"Are you lying?"

"Nope." He shakes his head. His eyes are still closed, but the corners of his mouth lift a bit.

"Oh yes, you are lying." I bend down slightly. "You just want me to pet you."

He opens his eyes and reaches up to tuck one of the strands that's escaped my ponytail behind my ear. "Yes," he says and closes his eyes again.

I take a deep breath, trying to control my racing heartbeat, and then bury my fingers in his hair. We stay like that, him lying on my lap and me petting him, in front of a turned-off TV until a phone ringing somewhere in Roman's room breaks the silence.

"Shit," Roman groans and sits up.

"I'll get it." I stand and hurry into his room.

When I come back, Roman is looking at me with strange intensity, but I shrug it off as one of the many strange looks he's been giving me lately and offer him the phone. He reaches for it, but instead of taking it, he closes his hand over my forearm and pulls me toward him. The phone is still ringing, but he doesn't let go of my forearm, drawing me between his legs. His other hand reaches up and rests at the side of my face, his thumb caressing my cheek.

"Roman?" I ask in a small voice, "What are you doing?"

"Answering the phone."

"It's stopped ringing."

"I know." His hand slides down my forearm and pries the phone from my fingers.

"Roman?"

"Yes, malysh?" He throws the phone to the side, and it slides along the polished floor all the way to the bookshelf.

My breathing quickens as I raise my arms and wrap them around his neck, then lean into him so that our lips are only millimeters apart. He doesn't take his eyes off mine, and the way he's looking at me does strange things to my insides.

"Are you trying to kiss me, Roman?" I whisper into his lips.

"I might be," he says.

"There's no one around to see us."

"Exactly," he whispers and touches his lips to mine.

He goes slowly at first, like he's savoring me, but then his arms close around my back and he leans back onto the cushions, taking me with him. The way this man kisses should be prohibited and ruled as hazardous to mental health. It feels like a hurricane is sweeping me off my feet, scrambling both my body and mind. I reach down with my hand, grab a fistful of his T-shirt and start tugging it upward. Roman breaks the kiss and removes his shirt at the same time I drop mine on the floor. While he's removing his sweats, I unclasp my bra and get rid of my leggings and underwear, and then climb onto his lap. His hand comes to the back of my neck, and he crashes his mouth to mine again.

I can't stop touching him, his chest, his face, his cock, which is already fully erect. Roman slides his hand between our bodies and I feel his fingers teasing my clit.

"So wet," he whispers in my ear and thrusts one finger inside of me.

I almost come on his hand right then and there, and I probably would have if he didn't remove his finger, making me growl in frustration. It isn't about his finger, though. It's about him. Roman Petrov, the man who will be my doom. Call it a premonition or an instinct—doesn't matter. I know he will destroy me because one look from Roman turns me on stronger than any other man before him has done with his cock.

"If you don't get inside me right this moment,"—I take a handful of his hair and squeeze—"I'm going to murder you, Roman."

His hands slowly travel down my chest and ribcage until he reaches my waist. Lifting me, he positions me above his cock, those devilish eyes never moving from mine, even for a second.

"Your wish is my command, Nina," he says and thrusts inside me.

I moan and hear him groan at the same time. He's too big but, dear God, it feels so good. I bury my nails into his shoulders as I spasm around him while he pounds into me. It's madness and I scream, not giving a fuck if anyone hears us. Roman groans my name and, a moment later, comes inside me. Perfection.

Roman's hand traces patterns from the top of my neck and all the way down to my ass, then backtracks upward. I've been lying sprawled over his chest for at least five minutes, but I can't make myself move.

"Nina? Everything okay?"

"Yeah," I sigh. "But I'm not moving. I like it here."

"I like having you here as well, malysh."

I wake to the sound of a fast tapping noise coming from some-where above my head. I stretch a little and open my eyes to find myself lying on the sofa with a pillow under my head and a blanket covering me from neck to foot. The lights are off and the TV in front of me is on, showing a news channel, but the sound is muted. The tapping sound stops and, in the next moment, I feel fingers combing through my hair. I tilt my head up and find Roman sitting at the end of the sofa next to my head. His hair is wet, and he has the laptop on his lap.

"You fell asleep on me earlier," he says.

"What time is it?"

"Half past seven. I told Varya we'll have dinner here when you wake up."

"Sounds good." I stand up, clutching the blanket around me. "I'm going to take a quick shower."

"All right. I'll tell the kitchen to send the dinner up," he says and returns to his typing.

I pivot and head toward my bedroom, feeling slightly awkward with the whole situation. We had sex. Where does that put us now? It's not just a business arrangement anymore, is it? Should we ignore the fact that we had sex and pretend it never happened? I'm not sure I can do that because, to be honest, I don't want to. We'll have to talk about it. I might be a fan of a shove-problems-under-the-carpet approach, but I don't think there's a rug large enough for it this time.

After my shower, I march back into the living room, intent on discussing the new situation with Roman, only to find him in his wheelchair, fully clothed, and putting on his wristwatch.

"What's going on?"

"Something came up. Don't wait up for me," he says, and before I can object, he's gone.

I stare at the door, then walk to the other side of the room where a big window overlooks the driveway. There are three cars parked in front, with four of the security guys waiting next to them. A couple of minutes later, Roman, Maxim, and Kostya come out of the house and get into the cars, followed by a few more security guys. And then, the cars leave.

Valentina brings dinner sometime later, but I leave it on the dining table, hoping Roman will come back soon. He doesn't, so around ten, I eat a few pieces of cold grilled fish and some salad. I put the leftovers into the fridge and watch some TV. Every fifteen minutes I get up and look out the window to see if the cars are back. Around midnight, I decide to call it a night.

The sound of shouting and car doors slamming wakes me. I jump out of bed and dash through the suite to the big window. Two of the cars are back. Most of the doors are open, and the last few men are coming inside. Two of them support the third between them, practically dragging him up the stairs.

Shit. I run back into my room, pull a hoodie and sweatpants over my pajamas, and rush toward the big stairwell.

There is no one in the hall. I turn around and notice blood splattered on the white marble floor, creating a path toward the right hallway, in the direction of the kitchen. I follow the

NEVA ALTAJ

red spots along the corridor and find the kitchen doors wide open. Urgent voices and a commotion blare from inside.

My blood runs cold at the sight of Varya hunched over Kostya. He is sprawled on his back on the big island in the middle of the kitchen, with Maxim holding a bloody rag to his side. One of the security guys comes running and places a box with medical supplies next to Kostya's head and then switches places with Maxim, who goes to the sink and washes his hands with mad speed.

They're all shouting in Russian, and I don't understand a thing they're saying, but the sight speaks for itself. Something went wrong. And where the hell is Roman?

Two more security guys burst into the kitchen with a short bony man carrying a doctor's bag. The doctor heads to the sink, and like Maxim, starts scrubbing his hands. They don sterile gloves and approach Kostya, who is pale, but conscious and panting. The doctor takes a look under the rag and prepares the needle and thread, while Maxim cleans the cut.

Footsteps approach from behind me, and the last of the security guys come into the kitchen with Roman wheeling in after them. A sigh of relief leaves my lungs when I see he's unharmed, and I lunge toward him.

"Jesus, Roman!" I whisper, grab onto his face with both hands, and kiss him. It's an angry kiss, but it still feels good. "What happened?"

"There was a slight disagreement with our supplier and things got out of hand."

"Kostya?"

"A knife slash on his side. He'll live."

I turn to look back at the island where the doctor seems

to be finishing sewing Kostya's side. Maxim is placing an IV needle in his arm, while Varya holds up the bag of fluid.

"Should I help with something?" I ask.

"No, let's go upstairs. Varya and Maxim have it under control, and the doctor will stay the night."

"Is it always like this? Deals going wrong, people getting stabbed or shot?" I ask as we enter the suite. I'm still shaking. "Or cars getting blown up?"

"Not always. But it happens."

My throat goes dry. How can he be so calm? In the kitchen, I grab a glass and pour cold water from the fridge. "That's fucked up, Roman." I shake my head and gulp down the water, wishing it was something stronger. "Your world is seriously fucked up."

"There's nothing I can do about it, Nina," he says.

Yeah, I guess that's one way to look at things. I should go back to bed but I'm too agitated, so I walk across the living room and stand at the window overlooking the driveway. The cars are gone. One security guy is standing on the side in front of the main door, a gun on his belt. Another one is patrolling the grounds toward the main gate, and this one has a rifle across his back. It looks like everything is back to normal in Roman's world.

I hear Roman approaching as he comes to stand behind me. His crutches enter my field of vision on either side while he hunches over me and places his chin on the top of my head. I've never felt so petite compared to him as I do with his huge body plastered to my back, but there's no panic. I guess all the adrenaline cured me of it.

"Where are we now, Roman?"

"What do you mean?"

"We had sex," I say, watching the man patrolling the grounds. "It wasn't something we planned for, you know. Where do we go from here?"

"I don't know, malysh. Where would you like to go?"

"I'm not sure."

There is silence while we both watch the night, its darkness broken by numerous lights set up around the lawn.

"It's late," Roman says and places a kiss on my shoulder. "Let's go to bed."

"Which one?"

"Well, I'll be in mine." He kisses the side of my neck. "And you can choose which one it will be for you. Your bed, or mine."

He leaves me standing at the window to consider his parting words. I know what I should do—go to my room and forget what happened on the sofa altogether. It would be the wisest choice. In fact, it should be the only choice.

I guess "wise" isn't in my cards. I turn around and head into Roman's room.

Roman

I watch Nina's sleeping form snuggled under the blanket, her hair tangled and sprawled across my pillow. The sight of her there, in my bed, makes a strange warm feeling fill my chest.

"Warren's here." I place a light kiss on her shoulder. "I'll be in the gym."

"Have fun," she mumbles into the pillow and continues sleeping.

Smiling, I get into my wheelchair and leave the room. She needs her sleep; we can continue where we left off later.

When I finish with my therapy session, Nina is still asleep, so I take a shower and go downstairs to my office. Maxim is already waiting for me, and by the look on his face, he has nothing pleasant to say.

"You need to invite the Albanians over, Roman. Soon."

"Not happening." I wheel myself behind my desk, power up my laptop, and start rummaging through the papers on my desk.

"I think you should reconsider."

"I'm not in a mood for entertaining Albanians."

"We need them as partners; you know that. You haven't met with them for months." He sits in the chair opposite me and leans forward. "They need to be assured that everything is in order."

"They're getting more money than in previous years, so I don't see why they would be concerned."

"If they don't feel we are invested as partners, they might turn to someone else, Roman. The last time I saw him, Tanush mentioned approaching the Italians. He put it as a joke, but he *is* thinking about it."

"Perfect. Just what I need." I toss the pen onto the papers on the desk.

Maxim leans back and crosses his arms. "So, who are we inviting?"

"Tanush and his wife. I think he's on the fifth one now. And Dushku and his wife. That's it."

"What about Hajdini?" he asks.

"No. He and Dushku are not on speaking terms lately. I don't need bloodshed."

"Alright. When?"

"Nina has her exhibition next weekend, so it'll have to be this Saturday."

"I'll let Tanush know." Maxim smiles. "Varya will be thrilled; she's just changed the rugs."

"I'll tell her it was your idea. Especially if it does end in bloodshed. Tanush might be a little hostile anyway, so make sure the men know."

Maxim raises an eyebrow. "Why? You two were always on good terms."

"We were on good terms, before I said I had no intention of marrying his daughter when he offered a few months ago."

Maxim lowers his head and regards me over the rim of his glasses. "And you're only telling me this now?"

If it was anyone else questioning my decisions, it wouldn't have ended well. Maxim, however, is the only person other than Varya I trust unconditionally. He's a father figure in a way my own never was. "I didn't find it important at the time."

"He inquired about Nina."

I look up at him. "And what did he want to know?"

"He asked if she was as beautiful as rumored."

That slimy bastard. "And what did you say to him?"

"I told him he can decide for himself when he sees her."

"Good. How's Kostya?"

"Lost some blood, but nothing serious. He'll be up and running in a few days."

"Keep him off for at least a week. Ivan can take over his duties till then. Make sure the doc comes to check up on him once a day until Monday."

"Anything else?"

"No. Go home. Rest. You've spent the whole night watching over Kostya. I'll have Varya take over."

When Maxim leaves, I call Nina. "Are you awake?"

"I am now." She yawns.

"Get ready and meet me downstairs in an hour. We have to go shopping."

"Oh?"

"I'm having some business partners coming over on Saturday for dinner. You need a dress."

"I definitely don't need another dress. I've purchased enough clothes to last me two lifetimes last week. Vova barely managed to get everything into the car, and I don't have any space left in the closet. There are at least ten dresses that I haven't even worn."

"You said you are an impulse buyer."

"That doesn't equal hoarder, Roman."

"We're still buying a dress."

"You like throwing money away? Is that some kind of compulsion? You can tell me, you know." She giggles.

No, I don't think I can tell her how much I enjoy buying things for her. "Don't make me wait."

"Hey, I need to walk Brando. He'll pee on the floor."

"Ask Olga to walk the beast."

"I'll tell Brando you complimented him."

"You can also tell him if I catch him chewing my laptop charger again, I'll be making you slippers out of his hide."

"Oh my God!" She bursts out laughing. "The big bad pakhan just made a joke. Are you feeling alright?"

I smirk. "One hour, Nina."

After cutting the line, I immerse myself in the reports Mikhail sent, as well as the plans for the next week's shipments. Though, thoughts of a certain black-haired woman prevent me from concentrating at all.

"How about this one?"

Nina exits the changing room in a little black dress. It has a high neckline with a hem that barely covers her ass. The cut is rather simple, however, the way it molds over her body and hugs her hips, emphasizing her tiny waist, is anything but. Combined with the strappy high heels and with her hair piled on top of her head, the result is devastating, and I find it hard to remove my gaze from her legs and her perky little ass. If she goes out into the street in that thing, she'll create a traffic disruption.

"We're buying it," I say in a strangled voice, "but find another one for the dinner."

"Why? What's wrong with it?" She looks into the mirror and cocks her head. "Is it too plain?"

"I'm not having my business partners ogling my wife's legs the whole evening."

"Don't be a caveman, Roman. It's not that short."

"You are not wearing that on Saturday." Or anywhere else in public, as far as I am concerned.

"Oh, for the love of God. Fine. I'll go find a potato sack instead."

I like the potato sack idea. In fact, if I could wrap her up from head to toe, it would make me very happy.

Nina ends up buying a pink midi dress instead, and while I'm not thrilled since it's low-cut and shows quite a bit of leg, it's much better than the black one. While she's taking a look at something on the blouse rack, I nod to the shop assistant to pack the black dress as well. After Ivan takes the bags, I take her to a jewelry store on the ground floor.

"No," she says when we stop in front of the window showcasing a multitude of necklaces. "I don't need jewelry."

She doesn't need it, that's for sure. When my little flower enters the room, she shines brighter than any diamond, but Tanush's and Dushku's wives will come covered in gold and jewels, and I don't want Nina to feel like she's anything less.

"Yes, you do," I say and take her inside.

She walks around the store, looking at the jewelry showcased in glass cases along the walls, until she comes to stand by the one that contains the most understated necklaces.

"How about this?" She points to a thin gold chain.

I ignore her and wheel myself to the big case on the opposite wall holding the best pieces. When the store attendant sees where I'm looking, he comes running and starts lining up the velvet boxes in front of me.

"I'm not wearing someone's house around my neck," Nina whispers in my ear.

"That one." I point at the set that consists of a necklace and a bracelet in white gold, lined with white diamonds, and look at the store attendant who is beaming at me—his eyes as huge as saucers. "And the matching earrings."

He nods eagerly and takes out another velvet box to place it next to the set.

"Yes." I nod. "Let's try them out first."

"Please tell me those are fake," Nina groans next to me, and I can't help but laugh. "They're not, are they?"

"No, malysh, they're not fake."

The attendant unclasps the necklace and comes to stand behind Nina, holding it up with the intention of putting it around her neck.

"Put your hands on my wife," I tell the idiot, "and you're losing them."

The man jumps and takes a step back, almost stumbling over his feet.

"Christ, Roman! What has gotten into you?" Nina stares at me with surprise, then turns toward the sales guy. "He doesn't mean that."

"I do. Turn around." I extend my hand to accept the necklace from the attendant.

After fastening it, I admire how it accentuates her slender neck. The bracelet is several sizes too big; she can probably put both of her wrists through it.

"We need this resized and delivered tomorrow." I give the bracelet back to the attendant, who nods eagerly, then I turn to Nina. "Do you want to leave the necklace on, or would you prefer they send it with the bracelet and the earrings?"

"I most certainly don't plan on walking around the mall with this thing on my neck. Can you please take it off?"

While I'm unclasping the necklace, I take the opportunity to run my fingers over the soft skin on her neck and notice her leaning slightly into my touch.

"Let's go home," I whisper in her ear. "You can try out those lacy thongs you bought."

She turns around and looks at me. There is hesitation

and concern in her eyes. "What are we doing, Roman? This. You and me. I-I have no idea what to think about all of this."

"Then don't think about it. Just . . . let go. Let the current lead us." I take her chin between my fingers and kiss her.

"Just let go?"

"Just let go, malysh."

"Okay."

CHAPTER
Ten

Nina

ALIGHT TOUCH OF A FINGER BETWEEN MY LEGS wakes me up. A kiss lands at the back of my neck, then another, a little lower. Roman's big body presses into me from behind, his arm coming around my stomach, plastering me to his hard, muscled chest. His hand slides to my pussy and starts circling my clit with one finger. When he slowly enters my core, I gasp, grab Roman's forearm, and start riding his finger. But he removes his hand. I turn around so I'm lying on my side facing him, throw one leg over his hip, and reach for his cock.

"Patience." He wraps an arm around my ribcage and raises me to sit on his stomach. Placing his hands behind my knees, he urges me up his body until I'm sitting on his breastbone.

"Roman?" I look down at him in surprise.

"You're not comfortable lying on your back. So, we improvise."

His hands trail up my thighs until he's gripping my butt

cheeks, and he ushers my body forward until his mouth is positioned just a few inches from my core.

"Hands on the headboard," he says, "and hold tight."

His mouth crashes into my pussy before I even have time to process his orders. I grab the headboard, my eyes rolling back into my head as he licks me, destroying me a little more with each swipe of his tongue. My mind is already half muddled, but when he sucks on my clit, it burns out completely.

I'm still shaking from the aftershocks when he lowers me down onto his chest. It takes me a few moments to come back to reality. I look up at him to find him watching me with a smug smile. Devious and dangerous, that's what he is. And he knows it.

I move lower until I feel his hard cock and rise to position myself over it. "Hands on the headboard, Roman."

His eyebrows raise, but he takes ahold of two of the wooden slats above his head. I smile and slowly start lowering myself onto his shaft, only to stop midway and lean down to kiss his inked chest. Then I lick it. Roman inhales deeply but doesn't move, keeping his hands on the slats. I wish I could tease him longer, but my core literally aches to have all of him inside, so I slide down slowly and close my eyes. Bliss.

"Do. Not. Move." I whisper and start rotating my hips.

While I ride him, Roman's hands grip the slats tighter, the muscles in his forearms straining. He wants to move, to thrust upward inside me. I see his desire and control in the intensity of his stare. There's something in his gaze, the way he's so focused on staying still because I've asked him to, that does me in. Roman Petrov is not a man who yields to anyone, but here he is, giving me the reins. A moan escapes my mouth as I come. Roman eventually loses his composure, and grabbing me around the waist, he starts pounding into me until I shatter.

As we lay with our limbs tangled, I trace my finger along the black lines on his inked chest. The designs are mostly abstract, similar to those in the full sleeve on his arm. What I failed to notice previously are the multiple scars scattered across his chest. I place my hand on one of the three on his right side. They appear more recent, breaking the flow of the black patterns.

"Those are from the car bomb," he says, caressing my back.

I move my hand to the left and touch the long thin scar above his hip.

"A knife fight on my sixteenth birthday. A discussion about politics that went too far."

Next, I pick a round scar on the left side of his stomach and circle my finger around it.

"Gunshot. Disagreement with Mendoza. He's the equivalent of a pakhan to the Mexicans, and things were a bit complicated back then. It was more than ten years ago."

I look up at him. "Ten? When did you take over from the previous pakhan?"

"Twelve years ago. When my father died, I took his place. I was twenty-three."

"How is that possible? You were so young."

"I started working with my father when I was fifteen. People supported me." He shrugs as if it's nothing. "It was a much better option than to have an internal war. Those are bad for business."

My eyes drift down to his chest, comprehension settling in as to how extremely different his world is from mine.

"What happened to Mikhail?" I ask.

Roman is silent for a few moments and then takes a deep breath and squeezes me to him.

"My father happened."

"Dear God. He . . . did that to him? Why?"

"It's a long story, malysh. A long and terrible story, and definitely not something I want to talk about in our bed. You'll have nightmares."

"That bad?"

"No. It's much worse than you could imagine, Nina."

Roman

My alarm goes off at seven. I look down at Nina who's sleeping on my chest and shake my head. I remember moving her down onto the pillows last night, but she decided to climb on me again at some point.

Trying my best not to wake her, I transfer her onto the sheets again and pull a cover over her naked body. We had sex three times last night, so she'll probably sleep in.

After placing a kiss on her shoulder peeking out from under the blanket, I get the crutches from where I leaned them on the nightstand and start getting ready for my appointment with Warren.

Somewhere in the middle of the session, Warren grabs the cane, which has been lying on a chair in the corner for a week, and brings it to me.

"Let's try this for a little bit," he says.

Slowly, I get down from the massage table and stand,

supporting my weight with my left leg and gripping the side of the table with my right hand.

"We'll start slow," he says. "Just a couple of steps for now."

I take a deep breath, hold the cane with my left hand and release the tight grip I have on the table. My first attempt is bad. The moment I raise my left leg to step forward, the searing pain shoots through my right knee so I almost stumble.

"Divide the weight between the cane and the leg. And try a smaller step this time."

It still hurts like a bitch, but it's slightly better. I manage a total of four steps before the pain becomes unbearable and I have to sit down. It's pathetic and I feel the need to hit something.

"That was good, Mr. Petrov," Warren says.

I raise my eyebrows at him. "If that was good, what's bad?"

"It's perfectly normal. You're putting almost all your weight on your injured leg for the first time in four months. Just the fact you can do that is very promising. I think you should switch to using forearm crutches from now on."

My body goes still. "I don't like those."

"Why? They require some practice but are much more convenient to use."

"Because they look . . . permanent." There. I said it. My greatest fear at the moment—that my knee is so fucked up, I'll end up walking on crutches for the rest of my life. A cane, I can live with. But I don't think I could bear crutches.

"They won't be permanent, Mr. Petrov. However, they're a much better choice for transitioning to the cane than the underarm crutches you've been using so far."

"Alright," I sigh. "When will I be able to ditch the wheel-chair altogether?"

"It depends. Your progress is much better than expected, and with enough practice, you should be able to manage using only the forearm crutches in a few weeks. But you should keep the wheelchair. You'll need it when we start practicing with the cane more extensively. Those sessions will put significant strain on your knee, and it would be better to use the chair in the following hour or two."

"Just get me to the bloody cane, Warren. I don't care what it takes, just get me there."

"I will, Mr. Petrov. Now, let's try those forearm crutches, shall we?"

Nina

The therapy session didn't go well. One look at Roman's face when he got back told me enough, and he barely said a word the whole morning.

I take the empty bowl I used for my cereal and go into the kitchen to put it into the sink. After filling up Brando's dish, I come to stand next to Roman.

"I was thinking," I say casually, watching him squeeze an orange, "maybe I could join you tomorrow when you're working out."

When Roman doesn't meet with his therapist, he spends two hours working out, and if he does have therapy, he exercises for at least an hour afterward. The man is seriously obsessed.

"Sure." He shrugs and starts pouring juice into the glasses. "What do you want to do? Treadmill?"

"I was thinking weightlifting."

His hand stills in the middle of pouring the juice, and he looks down at me with an incredulous look on the face, focusing on my nonexistent arm muscles. "Weightlifting?"

"Yeah."

"Alright." He bursts out laughing, and while I school my features to look offended, I'm smiling inside. His laughter is much better than his scowling face.

"What? It's popular. My Instagram feed is full of chicks with gym selfies. They say it does wonders for the butt muscles. Maybe I could take some pictures or even videos and upload them as well. I like those stretchy neon outfits and—"

In the next moment, I find myself sitting on the counter in front of Roman, who's holding my chin between his fingers and staring daggers at me. "No selfies in stretchy clothes."

"Oh, don't be such a grump. Everyone's posting those."

"My wife is not everyone."

Damn. It melts my insides every time he calls me that. And I secretly love his jealous streak. It's so cute. I lean in and straighten the collar of his shirt, then run my fingers through his still slightly wet hair.

"You are one disturbingly sexy man, Roman."

He breaks eye contact, looking down into his glass of juice. "Even with the crutches?"

Yup, that therapy session definitely didn't go well.

"Even with the crutches, Roman." I kiss him, and make sure to bite his lower lip just a little. "What did Warren say?"

"That I'm doing fucking great." Based on the way he's gritting his teeth, and the fact the knuckles on his hands are white from how hard he grips the crutches, their opinions differ quite a bit. "I have to go. I'll be back by dinner." He places a kiss on my forehead and leaves.

He's hurting. And it makes my chest hurt as well.

I sit on the counter for a long time after he's gone, looking down at the floor.

"Perfect," I mumble to myself. "Just perfect."

The head of the Russian criminal syndicate. A drug dealer. A killer. And I managed to fall in love with him. Someone please just lock me up in a mental institution, because that's apparently where I belong.

CHAPTER
eleven

I LOOK AROUND THE ABANDONED FACTORY WE sometimes use when setting up the deals, and curse. Three dead bodies lie sprawled on the floor, each one sporting a big red dot in the center of the forehead.

"What the fuck, Sergei?" I bark.

"They brought spoiled goods. What did you expect me to do?"

"To send them away, not kill them all. Damn it." I turn to Dimitri and Pavel who are checking the crates on the floor. "Get their car inside. Burn everything."

"The product as well?"

"Everything." I roll over to one of the dead guys and have a look at his face. "Mendoza's?" I ask and look at Sergei.

"No. Rivera's but working on their own. Probably stealing the product from Rivera, mixing it, and offering it under the table."

"We don't work with rogues, you know that."

"I was curious what they had to offer. The price was good." He shrugs his shoulders and lights a cigarette.

"Well, I'm glad you had your fun." I sneer. "Don't you dare pull shit like this again, you hear me, Sergei?"

"Yes, Pakhan."

"One more stunt like this, and you're done. The disadvantages of having you on the crew are running extremely close to exceeding the benefits. You get your shit together, fast. Find a bloody hobby or something."

I turn my wheelchair and leave, with Pavel following after me. This mess is not what I need today. If he wasn't my half brother, I would have gotten rid of Sergei long ago.

"Send him a hooker," I say to Pavel when we get into the car. "He needs to let off some steam."

"I already tried. He sent all of them away."

"How many?"

"Six."

"Try sending a male one." I don't think Sergei is gay, but I'm not sure.

"Yeah, that didn't go well, either." Pavel clears his throat. "He threw him out, then came to the club and broke my nose."

"Jesus, what am I going to do with him?"

"Counseling might help. Maybe the doc knows a shrink who wants extra money."

"The shrink would end up requiring counseling after talking to him, Pavel. I don't think anyone can help Sergei. He's a lost cause," I sigh and look through the window.

Nina

The bed dips next to me, and then I feel Roman's arm coming around my waist and his body spooning mine. I love when he does that.

"You missed dinner," I mumble into the pillow.

"I'm sorry, we had a situation. It's late, go back to sleep."

"Wake me up in the morning?"

"I will."

He kisses my neck and clutches me tightly into him. Falling asleep has never felt better, even with a headache.

"Malysh?"

"Hey," I groan. "What time is it?"

"Seven."

"Five more minutes." My head is killing me, so I just cover myself with the blanket, go back to sleep, and dream about being in school again. But then the dream transforms. I'm having sex with Roman, and we're in the middle of the deed when a guy with a knife comes out of nowhere and stabs Roman in his side. I jump up in bed, looking around. Other than Brando, who's playing with his ball in the corner of the room, I'm alone, and everything seems normal.

Feeling like a train has run over me, I drag myself into the kitchen, set the coffee to brew, and go to the bathroom. Showered and dressed in jeans and a top, I take out a bowl and prepare some breakfast. The clock on the wall shows noon, which means I have to be at my manicure appointment in an hour. A girl should doll up for her husband's business partners, but I'm too exhausted, so I call and cancel the appointment between two spoonsful of cereal. I'll play a trophy wife some other day. Maybe I should find Varya and see if she has something for my headache.

The moment I enter the kitchen downstairs, clinking silverware and clattering pots pierce right through my brain. I guess preparations for tonight's dinner are in full swing. Igor is shouting at Valentina and pointing at the stove. Varya is sitting at the table in the corner polishing the plates, but I can't stand the thought of subjecting myself to this chaos any longer. Roman probably has something. I leave the kitchen and head to the other side of the house.

I find Roman sitting behind his desk, its surface piled with paperwork. I never thought being the head of a crime organization would be so . . . bureaucratic.

"Do you have anything for a headache?" I ask from the doorway.

"Cupboard in my bathroom." He looks up. "Is everything okay?"

"I think I've caught a bug. Nothing serious."

Roman puts down the papers and motions me toward him with his hand. "Come here."

"I'm fine." I roll my eyes but go sit in his lap anyway.

"Do you have any other symptoms?" He puts his palm on my forehead and then on my cheek. "Take a pill and go lie down. I have to finish a few things here and then I'll come upstairs."

"I feel fine, Roman. It's just a headache."

He leans in and kisses me, and it makes everything feel a little bit better. Shit, I'm a goner for this man.

"Upstairs. Now, Nina."

"Well, since you asked so nicely." I kiss him quickly on the cheek and turn to drag myself back to my room.

 Roman

The lights are off when I enter my suite. I got carried away with work and almost forgot about the dinner. Dushku and Tanush will be arriving in an hour, and I expected to find Nina getting ready, but it looks like no one is here.

I turn on the lights and only then do I notice her lying on the sofa, curled up under a blanket. The dog is sleeping next to her feet. I wheel myself to the sofa and reach out to touch her face. She stirs and slowly opens her eyes.

"Is it time for dinner?" she mumbles and straightens to sit up. "I need to shower and get ready."

"You won't be going anywhere. You're burning up." I take the phone and call Varya, instructing her to bring a thermometer and Tylenol. "Lay down. I'll get you some water."

I head to the kitchen and bring a glass and a bottle of water from the fridge. Nina is lying down on the sofa again, her body curled up under the blanket and looking so small.

"I feel like someone chewed me up and spit me out," she mumbles. "I'm sorry, baby, but I don't think I can handle the dinner."

Something pierces me in the chest upon hearing the endearment. It's the first time she's done it without playing the part for the people around us. She probably didn't realize she said it, but it still counts.

The door opens behind me and Varya comes in, carrying a bottle of Tylenol. She sits down on the sofa and takes Nina's temperature.

"Go get ready." She motions with her hand. "The guests are arriving in less than an hour. I'll stay with her."

Tanush and Dushku arrive on time. I take them to the dining room and motion to the four seats on my left side. Tanush claims the chair closest to me, and his latest wife, who is probably his daughter's age, quietly sits down next to him. I pity the poor girl. Even under all her makeup and tons of jewelry, I can feel how scared she is. Dushku's wife is a different breed. Both taller and wider than her husband, she's rumored to handle all of her husband's financial matters.

Maxim and Dimitri are on my right, leaving the chair at my side empty. They know it's meant for Nina, and even though she's not joining us, neither one dares to take her spot. My idiot of an uncle, who arrives last, doesn't seem to have any sense left, because he walks directly toward Nina's seat. Fortunately for him, he raises his head just before he reaches for the chair. When he sees the look on my face, he quickly backtracks and takes the seat next to Dimitri.

I nod to Valentina and Olga, who approach the table and start pouring drinks. We've had these dinners quite often so they know the drill.

"And where is your young wife, Petrov?" Tanush asks while nursing his second whiskey.

"My wife is no concern of yours."

"Too bad. I was so excited about meeting her. To see for myself the girl who managed to nab the big bad Roman Petrov." He smiles. "The things I've heard, hmm . . . I wonder if she even exists."

I look at the bastard and wonder if I should gut him on the spot.

"The food's here," Maxim says, quite possibly saving the moron's life. "Let's eat, before the meat gets cold."

Olga rushes forward, setting the big plates in the middle of the table, while Valentina runs around refilling drinks. There's a steak knife beside the wine bottle. I reach for it and move it closer to my plate. Maxim excuses himself and leaves the table, but I don't pay attention to where he's going as my gaze is focused on Tanush. I have the feeling we'll be replacing the carpets again after all.

Nina

The pills started to kick in some twenty minutes ago, and I'm returning to normal. My head still hurts a little and my throat is sore, but it's eons better than this afternoon.

"I feel better. You should go downstairs," I say to Varya who hasn't left my side since she arrived.

"Roman said I'm to stay here until he's back, child. I have to message him every twenty minutes with updates or he'll come up."

"I'm fine. You have a ton of work to do tonight."

"If I go downstairs and Roman sees me, he'll get mad.

He's entertaining two very dangerous men, and he can't afford to be distracted."

Varya's phone rings. She reaches for it, looks at the screen, and tenses.

"It's Maxim," she says and takes the call. "What's wrong?"

She listens for a moment and shakes her head. "Absolutely not. She's had a fever for the whole afternoon . . . Alright." She extends the phone to me. "Maxim wants to talk to you."

I look at Varya, confused, and take the phone. "Yes?"

"Can you come down?" he asks.

"To the dinner?"

"Not for long, but yes. Please."

"Okay. I need to shower and change, though."

"How much time do you need?"

"Thirty minutes. Why?"

"I can't distract him for that long. Can you make it in fifteen?"

"What's going on, Maxim?"

There is a silence from the other end of the line, and then—

"I think Roman is going to kill Tanush, and we really don't need that now. I need him to focus on something else." He cuts the call.

I look at the phone, throw it at Varya's lap, and run straight to the bathroom.

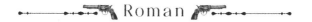

Roman

"You should have seen her, Leonid!" Tanush holds his hands in front of him. "Her hips were this big. I'm going to start manually approving all whores from now on. Can't offer un-tried goods to the clients, right?" He hits his leg and laughs like a madman at his stupid joke while his wife cowers on her chair, her face getting redder by the second.

When he comes up for air, Tanush continues, "Maybe that's why Roman rejected my daughter's hand in marriage? I guess I should have offered to let him try the goods first." He laughs again and turns to me. His face is flushed and his eyes watery.

I stopped counting his drinks after the fifth one, but I don't need to know how much he's had to see he's wasted.

"Your daughter is seventeen," I say.

"So what? My mother married at fifteen." He leans too close to my face. "Did you try out the goods before marriage? Tell me, was she good? Or maybe your cock got blasted along with your leg?"

I've had enough for tonight. I take the steak knife from the table, where I intentionally placed it earlier, grab Tanush by the collar of his shirt, and put the knife under his throat. Varya is going to kill me, but I will quite enjoy ending the bastard.

"My husband's cock works quite well, but thank you for your concern."

My head snaps up. Nina is standing in the doorway and looking at me with one eyebrow raised. She's wearing the short black dress, the one I said she wouldn't be wearing for this dinner.

"You have a fever. Get back to your room." I snap.

Tanush tries to wriggle free, so I press the blade into his neck some more, so it's just a hair's breadth shy of breaking the skin.

"I'm fine, honey. Can I join you? I see you've saved me a spot and I'm starving."

Nina approaches, her heel-clicks on the floor the only sound that can be heard and stops between me and the empty chair. After leaning forward to place a quick kiss on my cheek, she sits down.

"You must be Mr. Tanush. I've heard you own the biggest casino in the city. Maybe Roman can bring me one day and you could show us around, I've never been to a casino." She smiles at him sweetly and turns to me. "Honey, would you mind removing the knife? I'm trying to have a conversation here."

Tanush stares at her for a moment, then bursts out laughing. I slowly lower the knife, giving Dimitri a discreet signal to keep his gun ready, and let go of Tanush's shirt. He's still laughing. Crazy Albanians.

"I like her Roman! She's feisty, this one."

"Thank you, Mr. Tanush." Nina beams and I shake my head.

"This is my wife, Nina," I announce and send her an irritated stare. "And she definitely knows how to make an entrance."

"Thanks, honey." She brushes her hand over mine and turns to Tanush. "About that casino, how do you make sure people don't cheat? Do you have cameras that watch the tables or . . .?"

Tanush listens to Nina chattering and answers her questions. She's intentionally asking ridiculous things that make everyone snicker from time to time, keeping the atmosphere light. When she questions if the casino's air vents are covered by cameras, everyone looks at her and bursts out laughing as she explains that thieves in casino heists always get in through the vents in the movies.

She's in her element, playing her part of a naive and slightly slow-witted wife perfectly, but I can see the bags under her eyes, which she's tried to cover with makeup. It's clearly time to announce the end of this idiotic dinner and send the Albanians home.

Nina

When the door to Roman's suite closes behind me, I exhale slowly and finally let my shoulders slump. I feel like shit.

"Don't you ever do that again," Roman says through his teeth, and wheels toward me until I'm standing between his legs.

"What exactly?"

"Where do I fucking start?" he barks, his nostrils flaring. "You coming to a bloody dinner with a fever. Or putting yourself in harm's way. We were this close to full-blown bloodshed down there, and you walked right in the middle of it!"

"I'm sorry for distressing you."

Roman grinds his teeth. He's really mad.

"And you wore that dress." He leans forward and grabs me around the waist. "You're wearing that dress only for me from now on. Is that clear?"

I try my best to hide my grin. And fail.

"Alright, caveman." I put my hands around his neck and place a kiss on his mouth. "You're sweet, you know?"

"I'm not sweet, Nina. I'm fucking furious."

"Still . . ." I place a kiss on his brow, then another one on his hard jaw. "You're hot when you're mad."

"Are you trying to manipulate me?"

"Yes." Another kiss, this time on the other side of his jaw. "Is it working?"

"Maybe." He cups my face in his palms and slams his mouth to mine. "Get into bed. Your temperature is up again, I'll bring some Tylenol."

He is unbearable.

It's been three days since the dinner with the Albanians and Roman is still treating me like I should be bedridden. I found his mother hen act kind of cute on the first day, even though my fever broke, and I was back to normal. Now I just want to strangle him.

"I am not spending another day watching Netflix, and you're not working from the living room again." I poke a finger into his chest. "You will take your laptop and go downstairs to your office, and you'll do it now. I mean it Roman."

"The moment I'm out of the door, you're going to be up and working."

"I need to finish four more pieces in four days. Of course, I will be working. You made me spend three days on a sofa."

"You had a fever."

"Three days ago!" I throw my arms in the air and stare daggers at him. "I'm fine. Please, just go downstairs and let me work."

"Okay. But I *will* be checking up on you. If I catch you missing lunch again—"

"Thank you, Jesus."

He's following me with his eyes as I march to my work space and start prepping my paints on the table next to the easel. I'll have to buy more black paint as I'm down to my last tube, since I used most of my stash on the big guy. A few more tubes of red wouldn't hurt either. I've just dipped my brush in the paint when I feel Roman's lips land on the sensitive spot at the nape of my neck.

"You forgot something," he whispers and buries his face in my hair.

"Oh? And what might that be?"

"A kiss."

I drop the brush and slowly turn to find him looming over me. I don't flinch, and there's no feeling of panic. Having him this close, towering over me, stopped triggering me a while ago. I can't even pinpoint the exact moment it happened.

"You're so demanding." I cup his face in my hands and bring his lips to mine.

"I know." He kisses me again. "Make sure you eat some lunch. And, call me if you need anything."

When Roman leaves, I immerse myself in work, stopping only for bathroom breaks. By lunchtime, I have another piece done. Brando is getting restless; he's been running around for at least an hour and has now finally curled up in his dog bed. Maybe we could go for a walk and try our luck with getting into Leonid's room again. The last few times I tried, there was always someone around.

In my room, I take the small red ball and the black device from the nightstand, and whistle. Brando jumps up in his dog bed, and as soon as he sees the ball, he starts running around my legs. Placing the listening device in the back pocket of my jeans, I leave Roman's suite with Brando on my heels, and head into the west wing.

One of the maids exits Kostya's room just as I reach the elevator and, carrying a mop and cleaning supplies, unlocks Leonid's room and goes inside. Bingo.

I throw the ball toward the other end of the hallway and let Brando chase it for a few minutes. When I'm sure there's no one around, I take the ball from Brando and launch it right into Leonid's room. As expected, he dashes after the ball.

A mix of sounds start coming from the room. The maid crying out. Brando barking. Something hitting the ground. More barking.

"Brando," I call, but I don't expect him to come. When there's a ball involved, all his training vanishes. Very convenient.

I run into the room to find the maid cowering in the corner, holding the mop in front of her in a defensive stance. Brando ignores her completely and chases the ball below the small coffee table in the corner. I bend as if to get the ball and hit the table with my hip, which wobbles and tips to the side. A big glass bottle of liquor falls to the floor and smashes. Brando yelps and runs to hide under the bed.

"Get a dustpan and some rags, quickly," I say to the maid and kneel between the bed and closet as if trying to get the dog.

As soon as she's out of sight, I take the listening device from my pocket and look around. Most of the empty electricity sockets are in plain view, damn it. I almost decide to use one next to the overturned table when I notice an empty socket located between the closet and the dresser. No electricity devices nearby. It'll have to do. I reach with my hand and plug in the bug when I hear fast-approaching steps.

"Come on baby, it's okay. Come to Mommy," I coo, reaching under the bed for Brando.

"What are you doing here?" Leonid says from behind me.

I grab the spooked dog and stand up to face Roman's uncle, who stands at the doorway looking pissed.

"Oh, Brando ran inside chasing the ball and overturned the table. I am so sorry, Leonid. It won't happen again!"

He looks at Brando with disgust on his face and motions with his head toward the door.

"Get that animal out of here," he sneers.

I bend to collect the ball from the floor and then run out of the room.

Behind my back, Leonid mumbles, "Idiot."

Smiling, I return to Roman's suite.

Once inside, I let my lips stretch into a grin, take a bag with dog treats from the kitchen counter, and give Brando a double ration.

"Good boy."

CHAPTER
Twelve

A T LEAST A DOZEN DIFFERENT OUTFITS ARE sprawled over my bed as I consider which one to pick for tonight's exhibition. I barely managed to finish the last of the paintings in time. Mark almost had a heart attack when I told him I needed to make some changes on the big guy and wouldn't be sending it until this morning. He wailed for at least ten minutes about not being able to include it in the catalog. I prefer it that way. I want to watch Roman's reaction when he sees it for the first time.

Picking black leather pants and a green silky shirt, I drape them over the chair, and leave the rest of the clothes on the bed. I haven't slept in this room for quite some time anyway. All my things are here though, because other than sleeping in Roman's bed, I don't plan on moving in with him. Okay, that sounds really strange since, well, I do live with him.

"This is so weird," I mumble as I sit down at the vanity and start applying makeup.

My phone rings, and I take the call without checking the caller ID.

"Nina, is everything okay?"

If I'd known it was my mother, I would have let it ring. "Yes."

"You've been avoiding my calls for weeks."

"Again, yes. I don't see the point in this call, Mom."

She doesn't say anything for a few moments, and then surprises the hell out of me. "Your father and I would like to come to the gallery tonight. If that's okay with you?"

I look at my reflection in the mirror, wondering if I've heard her correctly. My mother's never come to my exhibitions. She once said that my art scares her.

"I'm not sure it's a good idea," I say finally.

"Why?"

"Well, first, this collection is rather dark. I don't want you to get a stomach ulcer. And second, Roman will be there."

"Yes, about your husband. I'm . . . I'm sorry for what I said the other day. It's just . . . I was surprised and I said some nasty things. It's hard to understand you sometimes, Nina."

I close my eyes and sigh. "I'm sorry I can't be the person you wish me to be, Mom. I never made it easy for you; I know that. But I am who I am. If you can't deal with it or accept my choices, that's okay. Just don't call me anymore. However, if you can accept my life and my choices without reproach and unnecessary commentary, you're welcome to come tonight."

"Okay, honey. We'll be there."

I end the call but stare at the phone in my hand. Why would she change her mind so suddenly? I scroll through my phone, find my father's number, and call him.

"Nina?"

"You told Mom, didn't you?" I ask.

"Yes."

"Jesus, Dad!" I slump in the chair and put my hand over my eyes.

"I had to tell her, Nina. She would've kept grilling you, so I told her to make her understand."

"To understand what?"

"Why you're with that man. I . . . I told her what I did, and that you married him because they would've killed me otherwise. I explained that you have to pretend."

"Well, I'm not."

"What?"

"I'm not pretending, Dad. I haven't been for quite some time," I sigh. "I'm in love with him."

"Nina! He's a killer. Are you crazy?"

"Maybe I am, but it doesn't matter. What does matter is that you will go and explain that to Mother. And if it doesn't sit well with the both of you, I don't want to see either of you tonight."

I press the end button, throw the phone in my purse, and go back to fixing my makeup.

Roman

I get closer to the painting and lean back, regarding it. The lights are muted throughout the gallery, leaving only a single wide spotlight above each painting to illuminate the space. It works well, considering the dark vibe of Nina's art. I had a look at most of the pieces while they were still at my place, but having them showcased in this way gives them a much more disturbing feel.

The painting in front of me shows a mirror reflection of a pale-skinned woman with long dark hair, holding a length of material clutched to her chest. In the space behind her, several faceless tall figures loom, their hands extended. Everything is done in shades of gray and black, except for the dress the woman is holding, which is bright green.

Before I move to the next piece, I throw a look toward the opposite corner of the room, where Nina is standing next to a short young man with a receding hairline. Mark, the "pimp". They're discussing something, and I pay attention to their body language for a few moments. Nina looks up and, when she notices me regarding her, smiles. She says something to Mark and walks toward me. I ogle her catlike body dressed in leather pants as she sways on sky-high heels. For someone who said they don't like wearing heels, she's managing quite well. Those things are ridiculous—at least five inches high, probably more.

"So, what do you think?" she asks and nods to the painting.

I take her hand, raise it to my lips and place a kiss at the top of her fingers. "They're amazing, malysh."

She smirks and leans toward me. "You're only saying that to drag me into your bed."

"You usually come to my bed of your own volition. But if you insist, I can drag you there myself tonight."

"I insist." She looks at me through hooded eyes and bites her lip—my little seductress.

"If you keep looking at me like that,"—I take her chin

between my fingers and pull her head toward me—"you'll miss your own exhibition, Nina."

"That doesn't sound bad at all, Pakhan."

I grab her around the waist and pull her into my lap. Nina laughs, wraps her arms around my neck and buries her fingers in my hair.

"I am taking you to say your goodbyes, and we're going home," I say and crush my mouth to hers.

"Can't," she whispers into my lips, "you haven't seen the big guy yet."

I growl at her.

"Seriously, Roman?" She kisses me again. "Animal sounds now? What will people think?"

"People can go fuck themselves."

In the corner of my eye, I see Samuel Grey approaching us warily, with his wife on his arm. "Your parents are here."

Nina looks up but doesn't make a move to get off my lap. Instead, she keeps playing with my hair while she watches them coming.

"Mr. Petrov," her father says when they approach. Her mother just nods, her eyes focused on Nina's hand which is still buried in my hair.

"Just Roman, please," I say and turn my gaze to Nina's mother. "So, what do you think about Nina's newest work, Zara?"

She blinks, visibly tense, then offers me a smile so fake it could have been plastered on Barbie.

"It's . . . nice," she says and looks at Nina. "We wanted to buy one of your paintings."

Nina stares blankly at her.

"Maybe something without dead chickens. If possible," her mother adds.

"You don't have to buy any," Nina says, still looking at her mother with slight confusion on her face. "Just pick the one you want and tell Sally. She's the woman in the red skirt standing at the entrance. Everything except the big one in the next room is for sale."

"We already asked when we came in," Samuel throws in. "She said all the paintings have already been sold."

"That can't be true, we just opened ten minutes ago," Nina mumbles and looks at me. "I have to see what's going on."

She climbs off my lap and hurries toward the woman on the other side of the room.

I turn to her mother. "Pick the one you like, and tell Sally I authorized it."

Zara Grey regards me with a surprise. "You bought them?"

"Of course, I did." I nod and look over at where Nina is standing with the curator. "Does your wife know, Samuel?"

He inhales sharply, and then lets out a strangled, "Yes."

"Good. But you should know something," I say and turn to face them. "The deal is off."

"Off?" He gulps and quickly clasps his trembling hands in front of him. "What does that mean?"

I study him, then move my gaze to Nina's mother who's staring at me with dread in her eyes. "It means I'm keeping your daughter."

Grabbing the wheels of my chair I head toward Nina, leaving her parents standing open-mouthed in front of a painting of a girl in the green dress.

"Sally says an anonymous buyer bought all the paintings!" Nina says the moment I approach.

I barely manage to keep my face straight. "What a selfish son of a bitch."

"Exactly." She nods. "Good thing I told Mark to note the big guy as not for sale right away."

"Why?"

She gives me a secretive smile. "That one is for you."

I stare at her, grinding my teeth. "Where is it?"

"In the other room, around the corner, but . . . where are you going, Roman, wait!"

I ignore her and keep wheeling my chair as fast as it would go toward the room she indicated. We agreed she wouldn't do the self-portrait for the exhibition, and I'll be damned if I was going to let anyone see it. They are taking it down right away, or I'm killing someone.

"Roman!" Nina's heels click behind me as she tries to follow. "It's not the one where I'm naked!" she shouts after me.

Suddenly, there's absolute silence in the gallery. I stop and turn to find at least fifteen people, including Nina's parents, staring at her with shock on their faces.

She doesn't seem to notice, and comes to stand in front of me, with her hands on her hips. "Why do you always need to make a scene?"

I raise my eyebrows. "You just informed the whole gallery there is a painting of you naked, and *I'm* the one making a scene?"

She blinks, looks over her shoulder at the people who are still staring at her, and snickers. "Oops."

"Yes." I nod my head. "Let's go see that painting before

147

I lose my shit, because there are at least ten men over there imagining you without clothes right now."

She giggles and motions toward her left. "This way."

We round the corner and enter a separate section of the gallery. It's almost as big as the first, but there's only one painting showcased here. Three spotlights illuminate it from above. The exhibition has just opened so there are only two people here. They're standing off to the side, which gives me an unobstructed view of the composition.

Like Nina's other works, it's done mostly in grays and black, but the shapes are sharper here, more recognizable. The whole bottom part shows piles of rocks, parts of buildings, and different debris. Clouds of smoke here and there are done in white paint. Above the central pile of debris, a lone figure sporting huge devil horns looms. He's also painted in black with shades of gray and holds a huge sledgehammer in his right hand as if he's in mid-swing. The figure's face isn't visible because he wears a huge red helmet in the shape of a wolf's jaws, and a long red cloak floats behind it. It's magnificent.

"Why is he smashing everything?" I ask, not able to move my eyes from the scene.

"Because he can, I guess."

"What's scattered around him? City ruins?"

"Not really. It's a metaphor."

"For what?" I ask.

Nina leans toward me and whispers in my ear, "For my poor demented mind. Or whatever's left of it after you've so skillfully demolished it, Roman."

My head snaps to the side and I stare at Nina, processing what she just said. I need her to elaborate, but she just stands there, looking at the painting. I hook a finger on the belt loop on her pants and turn her to face me. "Explain."

"You're a clever man, Roman. Think about it, and you'll come to the conclusion yourself." She kisses me and then turns toward Mark who's waving at her from the entrance, leaving me to stare at the painting in front of me.

❀ Nina ❀

"**A**NYTHING ON THE RECORDING FROM
Leonid's room?" I ask and turn on the mixer.
I've decided to make us piroshki for din-
ner. Roman says I'm trying to fatten him up. Like that could
happen with his workout schedule. I went to the gym one
morning and found him doing pull-ups, and boy was it a sight
to see. The man has a six-pack I previously believed could only
be achieved with a lot of photo editing. After that, I started
getting up at seven so I could make it to the gym by eight,
and drink my morning coffee while watching him. Since I've
started this routine, he rarely manages to finish an entire workout because I usually drag him to the bedroom. What can I
say? I get horny watching him work out. He doesn't com-
plain, so I guess he's okay with me stealing some of his time.

Roman has been in a sour mood for the last two weeks,
and I'm pretty sure it relates to not getting what he's after on
those recordings. I've not asked what he's specifically looking
to find, but I have my suspicions.

I feel a brush of lips at the nape of my neck, and then a kiss on my shoulder.

"Still nothing."

"You are sure your uncle is the one who tried to kill you?" I ask and his fingers go still on my neck. "It's so hard to guess, Roman."

"Yes. Which is why I don't want you anywhere near him unless I'm with you."

"What would he do with me? I'm . . . nobody."

What I mean to say is, "I'll be gone in a few months anyway," but I can't make myself say the words. It hurts too damn much to think about it, so I don't. I'm exceptionally good at ignoring things I don't find pleasant.

"You're my wife. Hurting you would mean hurting me."

Yeah. I guess having the pakhan's wife killed under his nose wouldn't paint a nice picture in the eyes of his partners and subordinates.

"I'll be cautious."

"Good." He kisses my shoulder again. "Leave that thing in the fridge. Get changed. I'm taking you to Ural."

"The mountain?"

"One of my clubs."

"One of . . . ?" I stare at him and laugh. "Man, I did good. I'm such a gold digger. My mom will be really happy when she hears."

"Why?"

"She's always advised me to marry well, among other things. I guess I can cross that one off the list."

"And what are the other things."

"Get a degree in economics. Not to bite my nails. Die my hair blonde."

"You're not touching your hair."

"Not a fan of blondes?"

"Not anymore." He bends until his nose touches mine. "Go get changed."

"The black dress?"

"Not if you have any intention of leaving this wing, Nina."

No more than thirty minutes to get ready is my usual MO. However, I decide to take it up a notch tonight, and spend fifteen more minutes applying makeup. I want to look my best in case we run into one of Roman's exes. It's vain, I know, but I don't care.

I find Roman in the kitchen. He's leaning on the counter, supporting himself with a crutch in his left hand and holding a tumbler of whiskey in the other.

His leg is getting better. He hasn't been using the wheelchair at all while he's in the suite for quite some time. Although, I still haven't seen him use the cane. I know he's practicing, but when I ask to see, he tells me he doesn't want me to see him wobbling around. It's stupid, but I don't press.

I look him up and down, loving how hot he is in black dress pants and a black dress shirt that molds to his body in the most sinful way.

"My oh my, someone is looking sexy tonight." I put my hands on his chest and straighten his shirt. "Where is your wheelchair?"

"No wheelchair tonight."

My eyes widen at his words. This is big. "Are you sure?"

"I'm sure."

I squeak with delight and kiss him.

"I'm so happy for you, baby." I remove a stray strand of hair from his forehead. "The guys are going to lose it when they see you!"

Olga sees Roman first and the expression on her face is priceless. She's on the other end of the hallway in front of Ivan's door when she hears us coming. Her eyes bulge, and the pile of pressed towels she's carrying in her arms falls to the floor.

I stifle a smile, trying to keep my face casual, and follow Roman into the elevator. His walking has improved immensely since he's switched to his new crutches. It's almost normal. Maybe a bit slower than it was before the accident, but it doesn't matter. I've seen what his knee looks like. It's a miracle he's come this far.

When we exit the elevator, Ivan and one of the security guys are walking from the direction of the kitchen. I guess they're coming with us tonight. They see Roman and freeze in mid-step. Ivan gathers himself first and approaches us.

"Pakhan. Nina Petrova." He nods and precedes to open the door.

With a side glance, I notice Valentina peeking around the corner on the other side of the hall, her mouth hanging open. There's no doubt that by the time we come back everyone will know the news.

The club is bigger than I expected, spanning the whole ground floor of a three-story glass building. It seems as if we've arrived too early because there are only a few people waiting outside; however, when the bouncers open the double glass doors for us and we enter, I'm surprised to find a significant crowd inside. Most of the people are gathered around tall tables along the sides of the space. I expect us to stop at one ourselves, but we cross the huge room to another set of doors. Two men are standing on either side and they open them as soon as we get closer. We're greeted the same way we were at the entrance.

"Pakhan," they say nodding to Roman and then me. "Mrs. Petrov."

I'm slightly confused by their behavior, because I didn't expect anyone to know about my existence.

This second space is smaller, but it's much more lavish. Instead of tall tables, five semi-circular booths are located around the room; two smaller ones on each side and a huge one, that could probably seat ten people, in the center of a small, raised platform. Ivan, who's been walking in front of us the whole time, walks toward the big booth and stands on the right side, his hands clasped behind his back. For a second, I worry about Roman taking the two steps onto the platform, but he manages without a problem. He turns and offers me his hand, and I step up after him. The security guy joins us on the left side of the booth, assuming the same position as Ivan.

"I feel strange," I whisper when I sit down next to Roman in the middle of the booth.

"Why are you whispering?"

"I don't know," I whisper again. "Why is everybody watching us?"

"Who cares," he says, grabs my chin, and kisses me.

 Roman

A man approaches Ivan and says something in his ear. He looks familiar, probably one of Pavel's men. Ivan nods and looks at me, but when I shake my head, he sends him away. I'm not in the mood for business tonight, he can pass the message to Pavel.

Nina sits snuggled into my side, a wine glass in her hand, watching the crowd. She's been talking nonstop since we came in, but she fell silent a few minutes ago. I wonder what's going on in that head of hers. She puzzles me—this strange little thing who's worked her way under my skin, bit by bit—ever since the moment I saw her for the first time in that hole of a restaurant. I wonder what'll happen when these six months elapse, and she realizes I have no intention of letting her go. Ever.

I raise my hand to trace the line of her bare shoulder, and then let it slide down to her delicate wrist. She looks so fragile, my Nina, but looks can be deceiving.

"Dance with me," I whisper in her ear.

Her head tilts up and those black eyes look straight at me, a question visible in them. She must wonder how the fuck she's going to dance with a man who can't even walk properly, but she doesn't ask, as I knew she wouldn't.

"Okay." She smiles.

"Give me your leg."

Curving her eyebrow, she turns toward me, crosses her legs, and places her right foot in my hand. Slowly, I remove her heel and place it on the seat on the other side of me, then let go of her ankle.

"Left."

"You should get some counseling, Roman. This foot fetish is getting out of hand." She laughs and switches her legs, and I repeat the action with her other heel.

I take one crutch, stand up, and take her hand in mine.

"Up, malysh. On the seat."

She giggles, climbs up to stand on the booth seat, and puts her arms around my neck. I smile. Even standing up there she's barely an inch taller than me.

"I like this setup." She kisses me. "From now on, I'm totally carrying a stool with me everywhere."

I place my hand on the small of her back and nuzzle her neck. She sighs and buries her fingers in my hair, and we stay standing like that while the sounds of a slow tune wind around us.

I'm not a fan of having my back turned to the crowd. I very much prefer the whole room in my sight, but I guess I'll have to rely on Ivan and Kolya to watch my back. And I like holding Nina like this, with my body disrupting the view from other men I've seen looking at her.

"How's the leg holding up?" she whispers in my ear.

"It's fine. Don't worry."

"Roman?"

"Yes?"

"I have a confession to make."

I kiss her shoulder. "Something bad?"

"Yeah. It's . . . well, it's a kind of a problem. A big one."

"Spill it, Nina."

She's silent for a few moments, and then makes my world tilt on its axis with six short words.

"I'm in love with you, Roman."

I close my eyes for a second and squeeze her tightly. It's like everything around me stopped.

"Then we share the same problem, malysh." I say into her neck, and feel her go still next to me.

When I raise my head and look at her, her lips are slightly quivering, and there are tears in the corners of her eyes.

"That six-month deal? It's off, Nina," I say and squeeze her waist. "I don't care what we agreed. You're mine now and I'm not letting you go. Ever."

 Nina

I place my palms on either side of Roman's face and search his eyes, which are looking into mine with such intensity.

"I'm not going anywhere, Roman."

"Promise me." He squeezes me to him, and for a moment, I find it hard to breathe. "Promise me, or I'm taking you home and tying you to my bed until you do."

"I promise." I run a finger along his jaw. "Should we sit back down?"

"No," he barks.

"Okaaay. Why not?" I ask, but he just grinds his teeth and says nothing. "Roman, is something wrong?"

"There are men here."

"It's a club. Of course, there are men here."

"They were ogling you."

I burst out laughing, but he just grinds his teeth some more. "Are you kidding?"

"Do you see me smiling, Nina?"

He's serious. "Roman, you're being unreasonable. I'm with you, am I not?" I place a kiss on his hard lips. "They can watch, but it's all they can do." Another kiss, on his brow this time. "Does that make it better?"

"Marginally."

I have no idea what's gotten into him, but I'm not letting him stand like this the whole night. He needs to get off that leg. I sigh and kiss him again. "Let's go home, baby."

Our car stops in front of the house at the same time as another one, and Leonid gets out of the back seat. He turns to meet us, his eyes snapping to Roman who stands next to me. It's dark, but there's enough light from the lamps to illuminate the shock on Leonid's face, which transforms to a look of pure hatred. He quickly schools his features into a pleasant expression and approaches us.

"Well, what an unexpected development. I'm so glad to see you back on your feet, Roman. Literally."

"Is that so, Uncle?" A corner of Roman's mouth curls up. His posture is relaxed, but I don't miss the way he's gripping his crutches. Despite how much his leg is hurting, he's doing a great job at pretending.

"Roman, I'm tired. Can we go up, please?" I say, then turn

to Leonid and smile sweetly. "I need to do my evening face routine before bed, and it takes at least an hour."

Leonid gives me a condescending look, then turns and marches inside the house. We follow him at a much slower pace.

As soon as the suite door closes behind us, I turn to Roman and point toward his bedroom.

"Bed. Now, Roman."

He doesn't argue with me, which is evidence enough that he's in a significant pain.

I take off my heels, and rush into the kitchen to grab his painkillers and a glass of water and take them to Roman's bedroom. He approaches the bed and then sits down with a stifled groan. In painful slow-motion, he raises his right leg onto the bed and reaches for the medicine bottle in my hand. After swallowing two pills, he starts unbuttoning his shirt.

"Let me," I say and take over.

He watches me in silence, then shrugs the shirt off and lies down on the bed. When I start unbuckling his belt, his hand covers mine and he shakes his head. "I'm sorry, malysh. Not tonight."

"Jesus, I'm not intending to have sex. I just need to see your leg."

"Just leave it. It'll pass."

I ignore him and continue removing his pants. Even though I'm trying my best to be gentle, he hisses in pain a few times. When I finally manage to get a look at his knee, I take a sharp breath. His knee is swollen to double its normal size.

"Shit, Roman."

I grab a pillow and carefully put it under his leg, trying my best to move it as little as possible. When it's done, I take off the fancy dress, put on one of Roman's T-shirts, and climb onto the bed to lie next to him. Covering us both with a blanket, I snuggle into Roman's side and put my hand on his bare chest.

"Nina, I need to ask you something."

The way he says it, in a strange, somehow detached tone, makes me look up and find him staring at the ceiling, his face set in hard lines.

"Okay," I say.

"If it ends up that the crutches are the best I can do, will you leave?"

I open my mouth to say how idiotic the question is, but he puts his hand over my lips, silencing me. He's still not looking at me.

"I need you to think about this before you answer. Think long and hard about what that means. I'll never be able to run, no matter how much progress I make. Stairs will always be a problem for me. You might be okay with it for now, but you're young. You'll meet other men who are not . . . damaged. Men who don't have limitations. So, if I have to use crutches for the rest of my life, and that's not something you can accept in the long run, I'll understand. I swear, I'll understand and there won't be any hard feelings on my side. But if that's the case, I need to know now. We can keep going until it works for us, and when it doesn't anymore . . . well, we can each go our separate ways. But I need to know. And I need you to be sure, Nina."

Roman's hand leaves my mouth. I try to get over the fact that he may find me so shallow, but then I look at it from his point of view, how I would feel if our roles were reversed, and I understand.

"Have you ever felt like I have a problem with that, Roman? So far, I mean."

"No. But you're an extremely talented actress, malysh. And from this point forward, I don't want that other woman, the one you created for the purpose of our agreement. No more acting, no more pretense."

"Fair deal. Okay then." I take a breath. "I would love to see you run or take the stairs two at a time. The cane is okay, I guess, and I'll be really happy if you come that far."

I know each word coming out of my mouth hurts him, because I feel him becoming so still it's frightening. God, I hate saying all this, but we need the issue resolved once and for all.

"If I could choose what I would love the most, it would be for you to go back to where you were before that bomb."

He's still looking straight up, but closes his eyes after hearing my words.

"But that's never going to happen, Roman. I know this is hard for you, and it tears me up inside. I would love to see you without the crutches, but only because I know that's what would make you happy. That's the only reason. I love you, and I want you happy. I want that for you, so, so much." I take his face in my hands and make him look at me. "As far as I'm concerned, it doesn't matter. With or without crutches, I love you the same, baby. Even if you have to go back to using the wheelchair. I don't care. I don't give a fuck, Roman. The only thing I want, is you. Can I have you, please?"

"You already have me, malysh." He kisses the top of my head.

There's only silence after that. He isn't convinced. I want to cry so damn much, but I somehow manage to keep myself together.

"Tell me, Roman, wouldn't you love for us to be able to have sex in the normal way? Because I would. I would love nothing more than to have you above me, to feel your body pressing against mine, pulling my hands above my head. Well, that's not in the cards for me, for the foreseeable future at least. Maybe forever. Is that a problem? Will you get bored with my issues, decide to swap me with a less faulty version at some point? A woman who won't involuntarily flinch when you approach her from behind unannounced? Or someone who won't have a panic attack when you forget, and grab her wrist instead of her forearm?

"Do you think I haven't noticed it's always Dimitri or Ivan coming with us, never Kostya or Mikhail, or Sergei, who are all as tall as you? Or how they either sit down or leave the room when I come in? When I went into the kitchen a few days after Kostya was stabbed, he dropped down into the chair so abruptly, it's a wonder he didn't tear out his stitches. You had to instruct your men to fucking sit down when I enter a room so I wouldn't freak out. I'm sure it's tiring and frustrating, dealing with my issues. Will you decide to have me replaced with someone less fucked up at some point?"

"Christ, Nina." He stares at me in shock. "How can you say something like that?"

"Oh, you don't like how that sounds, huh? Well, fuck you, Roman," I whisper, turn my face into his chest, and let the tears fall freely.

I feel his hand in my hair, his other arm coming around my waist, and in the next moment, he has me lying on top of him. He removes the strands of hair stuck to my teary face, and brushes the skin under my eyes with his thumbs.

"I'm so sorry, milaya. It's just . . . I love you so bloody much. I'm scared shitless that you might walk away one day."

I grind my teeth. "Give me your hand."

He raises his eyebrow, but does as I ask.

I lead his hand down between our bodies until it reaches between my legs, and I press his fingers over my wet panties. "You feel that, Roman? That's what only lying next to you does to me. I'm so crazy about you, baby, that simply being close to you makes me dripping wet," I whisper, and I feel him getting hard under me.

Slowly, he hooks his finger in the waistband of my panties and starts dragging them down.

"Off," he barks.

"Roman, no . . ."

His other hand grabs them, and there's a sudden sound of fabric tearing. I'm still stunned over the fact he just tore my panties off me when he pushes his boxer briefs down, grabs me around the waist, and slides me down his cock. It feels so good that my eyes roll in my head, while my muscles start spasming around his length.

"Mine," he utters and slams into me. "Only mine. Say it."

"Only yours, baby."

Another slam and I'm done, my insides imploding. Shudders overtake my body. Roman groans as he thrusts deep inside me, and I feel his seed filling me. Still coming down from the high, I drop onto his chest. That was the most mind-blowing one-minute sex I've ever experienced.

Roman's arms come around my back, squeezing me to him, and I feel his lips kiss the top of my head.

"So, you're staying for good?" he whispers.

"You're not getting rid of me even if you try. I'll never be able to find such a sexy husband again." I smile and kiss him. "We're closing this subject, Roman. Deal?"

"Deal. But I need you to know one thing. When I find the bastard who hurt you, I'm killing him."

"No, you're not." I squeeze his arm. "I don't want to have anyone's death on my conscience, so please, I beg you, forget about it."

"Nina . . ."

"Please, we're closing that subject, as well. You are not killing anyone for me. I can't live with that. Please."

When he doesn't reply, I take his face in my palms and press my forehead to his.

"You won't do that to me. You won't seek him out, and you won't kill him. If you love me, you won't make me bear anyone's death on my soul. Say you understand, Roman."

There's silence and then, "Okay."

CHAPTER
fourteen

Roman

MY KNEE IS MUCH BETTER THE FOLLOWING morning, but it still hurts like hell when I place any weight on my right leg. After breakfast, I ditch the crutches and take the wheelchair. I haven't been using it for weeks, and I hate that I have to now, but I don't want to risk any further damage to my knee. Nina may not have a problem with me using the crutches, but I do. Whatever it takes, I'm getting to that damn cane, because I want to be able to hold her hand in mine when I'm taking her to dinner, or even just for a walk.

"I'm going downstairs. Igor is teaching me to make *borsch*." Nina smiles, leans in, and kisses me. "Want me to bring lunch when I come back?"

"Yeah, I'll be working from here. And tell that boar that if he dares to raise his voice to my wife again, he's done."

"Don't be an ogre, Roman."

I watch her leave, then go to my bedroom and turn on the laptop. Bringing up the audio software, I find the recording from Leonid's room and play the feed at the approximate moment we came back last night.

There was a specific reason for me hiding the fact my leg is getting better. I'm almost positive that seeing me walking again will lead Leonid into trying something, and I want to catch his partner before that. It's been almost five months, and since I've failed to find out who the motherfucker is, it's time to nudge Leonid into action. Based on the way he stared at me last night, I have a feeling there is a nice surprise waiting for me.

In the middle of the recording, I finally find what I am looking for. Leonid is calling someone, and since the timestamp at the corner of the screen shows two a.m., I'm pretty sure it's not a business-related call. What surprises me though, is the person who answers.

"We need to try again. That bastard is walking," Leonid says.

"Hm. I'm not sure it works for me anymore, Leonid," answers Tanush.

"You can't change your mind now!"

"Of course, I can. I acted impulsively. I was mad because Petrov rejected my daughter, and I wanted to make him pay. But he makes me good money."

"We had a deal, Tanush. You help me take him out of the picture, and I make sure you get a better cut when I take over."

"See, that's the thing, Leonid. Even if you give me a bigger cut, I doubt you can keep the business going. I've decided I don't want to risk it. I'm out."

The line goes dead.

I lean back in my chair, take my phone, and call Maxim. "Where's Leonid?"

"He's out. I heard him tell Valentina to bring him his dinner up at five."

"That won't be necessary. I want everyone off the upper floor after four. And I mean everyone. No one comes up until I give word."

There's silence on the other side, and I presume Maxim's connecting the dots.

"I'll make sure it's done. What about Nina?"

"I need her out of the house. Dushku's daughter is getting married, and he's invited us to attend. I'll send her to shop for a gift. Tell Dimitri to send Ivan with her. They're not to come back under any circumstances before I call him. I don't care what he needs to do to distract her, she's not coming back here until I'm done. Is that clear?"

"Yes, Pakhan."

It takes some convincing, but I manage to send Nina away at around four p.m. She was hellbent on us having dinner together, but she caved when I said I have too much work to do.

I enter my walk-in closet and take my gun. After checking it, I grab my crutches and head into Leonid's room. I sit in the recliner in the corner, directly across from the door, place the gun on the coffee table, and wait.

Sometime before five p.m., Leonid enters the room. Seeing me there, his eyebrows shoot up, but he collects himself rather quickly. "Something happened?"

"Close the door, Leonid."

"Roman?"

"The door," I say.

He does as he's told and starts walking toward me when he notices the gun on the table. He stills, eyes going wide, then turns to run away. I take the gun and, pointing to his right knee, I shoot.

The sound explodes in the room, and Leonid's scream follows. He crumbles to the floor on his side and starts wailing, clutching his bloodied leg.

"If you wanted to take my place, you really should have made sure I was dead, Leonid."

"Bastard," he sneers through his teeth, his spit flying everywhere. "I'm going to kill you!"

Screaming, he lurches in my direction, his hands raised like a madman's. I aim at his head and let the bullet fly. His body crumbles to the floor, blood pooling around his head.

"You had your chance for that, Uncle," I say to his prone body.

I stand up and start walking toward the door when Leonid's phone rings. I consider ignoring it, but then bend down and reach for it, as my knee screams in pain. The screen shows an unknown number. I take the call.

"I found her," the voice from the other side says. "Prepare the money transfer."

The call disconnects.

 Nina

"Are you sure?" I look over the vase I'm holding. "It's atrocious. I'm positive they'll love it, and this one already costs more than a car."

"Pakhan said it needs to be something large." Ivan shrugs his shoulders and stands behind me.

"I'll ask if they have bigger vases." I turn toward the sales assistant.

I feel overwhelmed with all the fancy pieces of décor on display around me. It makes me nervous knowing the cheapest item here has at least three zeros on the price tag. There are more appropriate things that can be bought as a wedding gift, but for some reason, Roman insisted I come all the way across Chicago and choose something from this exact shop. Everything here is so over the top, including the golden chandeliers and life-size *David* replicas. It makes me shudder. Some people have really strange tastes.

I pass the tall glass vitrine holding sets of crystal glasses when I hear a sound piercing the air. The vitrine shatters and falls to the ground, a million tiny glass pieces exploding everywhere. People start screaming. Hands grab me around the waist and pull me down to the floor. In the next moment, Ivan is hunched over me, ushering me toward the back of the store. Another shot rings out and I stumble, reaching with my hand to avoid hitting the floor headfirst. Pain sears my palm. With his hand clutched around my upper arm, Ivan drags me toward the emergency exit, while shouting into the phone he holds with his other hand.

We burst through the emergency exit into the back alley at the same moment a car comes around the corner. The tires screech when the car stops abruptly. Ivan pushes me back inside the doorway, reaches into his jacket, and takes out a gun. I hear two shots ring out almost simultaneously.

"Stay there," he says over his shoulder and leaves my sight.

A couple of seconds later, I hear another shot. I have no idea what's happening. Is it a random shooting or is someone trying to kill us? Should I stay here or go back inside? Should I get out and look for Ivan? I'm so scared, I'm not sure I could move from the spot even if I knew where I should go.

I look down at my left hand where a big chunk of glass is half-buried in my palm, blood pooling around it. It hurts like hell.

Footsteps are coming from the alley, fast, so I take a deep breath and wait to see who it is.

Ivan enters my line of sight, grabs my hand, and takes me running down the street. I throw a look over my shoulder and see the car. The driver's door is wide open and an unmoving figure lies on the ground. Sirens blare somewhere in the distance, but the sound is nearing.

My steps falter, but Ivan keeps dragging me down the street and then around the corner toward the parking lot where he parked our car.

He opens the door and is ushering me inside when he sees my hand and hisses.

"Nina Petrova! Dear God, why didn't you say anything?"

"Didn't seem like a priority back there," I say and raise my hand. "Do you think the doctor who patched up Kostya would do the same for me?"

Ivan raises his head to stare at me with wide eyes, then shakes his head and murmurs something in Russian. "We're going to a hospital. If we don't, Pakhan will not be pleased."

"I guess we shouldn't rattle his cage. Your pakhan has been a bit cranky lately. Let's go then."

Ivan snorts and helps me inside the car, and we leave.

 Roman

"There's been a shooting, Roman."

I stare at Dimitri and swear my heart stops beating when the call from earlier flashes through my mind. No. I grab for his throat and bring my face to his.

"Where is my wife?" I sneer through clenched teeth, trying my best to keep myself from breaking his neck.

"We don't know. Ivan called to say that someone started shooting when they were in the store, and that he's getting her out. That was fifteen minutes ago. I can't reach him; he hasn't been answering his phone since."

"The others?"

"There's only Ivan. I instructed two of the security team to go with them, but Nina Petrova said she didn't want them with her."

I grind my teeth and squeeze Dimitri's neck until he starts turning red in the face.

"If there's a single strand of her hair harmed, there will be a lot of dead people," I bite out. "Starting with my head of security, who sent my wife out with only one man as her security detail. You got that, Dimitri?"

"Yes, Pakhan."

"Good. Now, get me a fucking car."

Nina

Three butterfly bandages, a tetanus shot, and a bottle of anti-biotics. That's what I got. Not even stitches. The nurse said I was lucky, and should take more care with washing the glasses next time.

I look up, trying to locate Ivan. Hopefully, he'll be here soon so we can get back home already.

There's a bang, the door opens, and raised voices come from the direction of the entry hall. I wonder if they're bringing someone seriously injured because the shouting is particularly loud. And then I hear Roman's voice roaring.

"Where is my wife?"

Crap. I was hoping we'd get back to the house before he found out what happened.

"What's happening out there?" The nurse who's been collecting her supplies murmurs and looks toward the sound of the voices.

"Aah, that would be my husband." I offer her an innocent smile, jump down from the gurney, and run from the room.

When I reach the reception area, I see Roman towering over a bald middle-aged attendant who's trying to type something on the keyboard. His hands are shaking so badly, he can't manage to hit the right buttons. The only other person in a ten-foot radius is Dimitri. A couple of other people present are standing next to the wall, keeping a safe distance. Ivan enters from the other hallway only to stop in his tracks upon seeing Roman in a rage.

"Roman?" I say.

His head snaps in my direction and he inhales a big breath while watching me approach. Slowly his gaze travels from my head, down my body, to the tips of my toes peeking out of my heels, and then up again. Only then does he exhale.

He grabs me around the waist and crushes my body to his. "You're never again leaving the house without me," he whispers in my ear. "Never."

I want to tell him what nonsense that is, but then change my mind. His body is strangely tense next to mine, and I notice that his hand on my waist is trembling slightly. He's really mad.

"Okay, baby. Sure. Let's go home, yeah?"

Roman just nods, passes his right crutch to Dimitri, takes my hand, and starts walking toward the exit. I take a look at our joined hands, but quickly look up and focus on the car parked some distance away. My eyes fill with happy tears as I adjust my pace to match Roman's.

Chapter Fifteen

Nina

"WHERE'S LEONID?" I ASK ROMAN DURING breakfast. "I haven't seen him for two weeks, and last evening, I saw the guys taking out his things."

"He's gone." He reaches with his hand and takes his orange juice.

"Gone, like he doesn't live here anymore?"

"You could say so."

"Roman?"

"Yes, malysh?" He looks at me and stuffs the fork piled with scrambled eggs in his mouth.

"You killed him, didn't you?"

"Of course, I did."

I choke on the piece of bread I just put in my mouth and reach for the water. "You cannot tell me that kind of shit during breakfast, Roman."

"You asked. And he tried to kill me first."

"So that makes it okay?"

"He was planning round number two. Does that fact make it more bearable for you?"

"I guess." I think about Leonid trying to kill Roman again and conclude that I would probably kill him myself in that case. "Yes. Nobody tries to kill my husband and gets away with it. You made the right choice."

"I'm glad you approve."

"I do not approve of killing people. I just . . . I can live with it in this case."

"You have really strange views, Nina."

"Since I'm living in your strange world, I guess it's fitting." I look at the clock and jump up from the chair. "We're going to be late for the wedding."

"What are you wearing?"

I smile mischievously, take a fistful of his shirt, and pull him toward me. "You'll have to wait and see."

I kiss him and start to pull back, but he grabs me around my waist and drags me into his arms.

"If you play with fire, my little flower," he says in my ear while his hands hook around the waistband of my jeans and start pulling them down, "you may get burned."

"We'll be late."

"Do you think I care?"

Nope. And I don't either. "How durable are those chairs?"

"Let's find out."

While he takes off his sweatpants, I remove my jeans and underwear and climb onto his lap.

My legs are too short and dangle on either side. Even

when I stretch, I can't touch the ground with my toes. "I don't think this will work, Roman."

He looks down, failing to stifle his laugh. "Jesus, Nina. You're so tiny."

"Should we move to the bed?"

Roman tilts his head to the side, and leaning back in the chair, he grabs my waist while his lips curl in a smug smile. "Nope."

My eyes widen as he lifts me up and positions me above his hard cock then lowers me onto it. I gasp and clutch his shoulders, loving the way he fills me gradually. A moan escapes me when I feel him fully buried inside. Roman's hands move lower, beneath my thighs, and he lifts me up then slides me down, impaling me again and again as I pant and hold tightly onto him. I'm not sure what turns me on more: the way his cock slides in and out of me, or the ease with which he handles my body as if I weigh nothing at all. He slams into me one last time and I come, hearing him groan as his seed fills me.

"Everything okay?" he wraps his arms around me and presses me into his chest.

"Yeah." I bury my nose into his neck, inhaling his scent. "I want random chairs to be put in every room. That bench-press machine you have can go."

"You weigh half the weight I usually lift, malysh."

"They say it's more effective to work with less weight, but more often."

"Do they?" His hands caress my back, gliding downward until they reach my ass. "I like that new workout plan. A lot," he says and squeezes my butt cheeks.

The wedding is extremely boring. Tons of guests are milling around with glasses in their hands, chatting and fake smiling. I don't know a single person here, so I spend most of the time people watching and commenting on their outfits to Roman. He always finds my babbling amusing. However, a few minutes ago he got stuck in a conversation about politics with some men, and I decide to leave him to it and go to sit at one of the tables.

I don't have a problem with sitting alone, but it seems like some people think I do, because a couple of women sit with me and drag me into a tactless conversation about who bought what for the newlyweds.

"We couldn't come with anything meaningless, you know," a pretty blonde with pumped lips explains. "I'm sure they'll enjoy the weekend at the spa. It's a highly exclusive place. Please don't ask how much we paid for reservation; the amount was atrocious."

"They'll love it." I smile.

"And what did you get them, dear?"

"An extremely ugly vase," I say. "My husband insisted on it."

"Oh, well, maybe your tastes differ. And which one is your husband?"

I look over to the group of men in the middle of the hall and smile. "The sexiest one in the room," I declare.

"You're biased." The other one, with a short red dress and red hair, laughs.

"Nope. It's a fact." I shrug.

They both turn to look at the mass of people like they're trying to guess which one would that be.

"The one in a brown suit, yes? The one with the glasses?"

I follow her gaze and see a shortish guy who's rather handsome, and has an accountant feel around him. I smile widely. This will be fun.

"Nope. Try again."

Next, she points out a man in a tuxedo. He's kind of cute and has longish hair but is way too thin. However, before I have the opportunity to answer, the blonde interferes.

"Oh my God, Sandra, is that Roman Petrov?" she exclaims and grabs for the redhead's forearm. Nodding toward the crowd, she asks, "What happened to him?"

"I think Rory mentioned he had an accident a few months back," Sandra whispers and turns to her friend. "I heard he got married."

"No! Where's his wife? What does she look like? Is she Russian?"

I raise the glass to my lips to hide my grin and continue listening.

"I haven't seen her. Probably tall and platinum blonde. That's his type," Sandra says.

"Well, she must be some harpy if she had the balls to marry him."

"Oh, she's a harpy, believe me," I throw in.

Both women turn to stare at me with wide eyes.

"You know Petrov's wife?" Sandra leans over the table, basically pushing her face into mine.

"Yup." I nod and take a sip of my drink. "She's a little whacky in the head."

"Well, she must be if she married him. No one in their

right mind would marry the Russian Mafia's pakhan." She tosses another look at Roman. "I heard Dushku say he almost sliced Tanush's neck during dinner last month."

I'm quite enjoying the situation when Roman ruins my fun. He turns his head and looks directly at me, a barely visible tilt on his lips. I raise my hand and blow him a kiss. Roman sends me a really heated look, and then goes back to his conversation. I turn back to find both women watching me with horror on their faces.

"That one is mine." I grin. "I'm Nina Petrova. The harpy."

They both smile, quickly excuse themselves, and are gone in seconds. I reach for my glass, take another sip of the wine, and resume people watching.

A woman approaches Roman's group and joins the conversation. I don't pay much attention to her at first, but a few minutes later I notice her discreetly move to stand closer to Roman and ask him something, a smile on her face. She's classically beautiful, with brunette hair twisted in a bun at her nape. A long beige dress is plastered to her body. Her head reaches Roman's shoulders, which puts her at least a head taller than me. She laughs at something and bats her eyelashes. I don't like the way she looks at Roman. He doesn't pay attention to her at all, but still . . . I wonder if I should go over there and send her packing. Maybe not.

I cross my legs, making sure the slit on my dress reveals them, and sit more comfortably in the chair. Roman looks in my direction, and I send him the secret little smile I like giving him before I drag him into bed. His eyes narrow. The woman is saying something to him, but I hold his gaze and lift my hand to run a finger across my lips. I cock my head to the side a little, let my finger slide down my chin and neck slowly, and stop at the neckline of my low-cut dress. Roman is following my finger's path, and when his eyes snap back to mine, I smile widely.

He says something to the people around him and starts in my direction, never once breaking his gaze from mine.

"You called?" His lips lift at the corners.

I stand up, put my hand on his chest and look up at him. "You are not the only one who's territorial in this relationship, Pakhan."

"Jealous? Of whom, malysh? You know there's only one woman my eyes see."

"Is that so?" I hook my finger into his shirt between the two buttons and pull on it until he bends his head and our noses touch.

"Staking your claim, Nina?"

"Of course I am, Roman," I say and kiss him.

"Home," he whispers into my lips. "Now."

 Roman

"I made you something."

I look up from my desk and find Nina's head peeking around the door. "Did you burn it?"

"It's morozhenoe." She beams, comes to stand between my legs, and fills a spoon with the ice cream from the bowl she's holding.

I watch her raise the spoon to my mouth, then lean in and let her feed it to me.

"Igor has been teaching me some Russian," she declares.

"Oh, I can't wait to hear what you've learned."

"We covered *govno*, *chort vozmi*, and *skotina* so far. Those are his favorites."

"I don't doubt it." I reach for my phone and dial Varya, who answers after the second ring. "Igor has been teaching Nina to curse. Does he have a death wish again?"

"Roman!" Nina grabs my shirt and reaches for the phone, but I move my hand away and kiss her instead.

"No one will be teaching you Russian, but me. Got that?"

"Got it, *kotik*."

I close my eyes and shake my head. "You do not call a Russian pakhan 'kitten', Nina. I have an image to uphold here."

She narrows her eyes at me, schools her features to embody seriousness, and touches my nose with her finger.

"My deadly kotik. Better?"

"Nope."

"You're no fun." She winds her hands around my neck. "Let's go somewhere for dinner, hmm?"

"I'm sorry, malysh, I have some business crap to deal with tonight. We leave in twenty minutes, and I don't know how long it'll take, but I should probably be back by ten or eleven."

"Be careful, Roman."

I watch her leave and think how strange it is to have someone waiting for me to come back from work or worry about my well-being.

 Nina

Roman still hasn't come back. I clutch my sweater tighter around me and look at the clock again, probably for the hundredth time in the past hour. It's half past three in the morning, and he hasn't called or texted. I didn't want to call him and intrude on his business deal, so I checked with Maxim—who stayed at the house—around one a.m., then again around three a.m. He didn't know anything.

"Damn it, Roman," I murmur to myself, eyes glued to the gate visible on the other side of the lawn. "Don't you dare get yourself killed."

Sometime around four a.m., the gate slides to the side and two cars park in front of the house. Men start exiting the cars, and I plaster my palms onto the window, looking for Roman. He exits last, and the way he gets out of the car—painfully and slowly—tells me he's pushed his knee way too far this time.

"Stubborn, stubborn idiot," I mumble. A distance he usually covers in seconds now takes him almost five minutes.

What the hell was he thinking? Warren told him he wasn't allowed to walk long distances for at least a few more weeks, and he goes and pulls an all-nighter not even a week later.

In the bedroom, I take out the wheelchair from where he stowed it in the wardrobe, and park it just next to the door. He has this moronic idea that he won't let his men see him in the chair ever again, so I cross my arms in front of me and wait for him.

Ten minutes later, the door opens, and he hobbles inside. He looks at the chair, then at me. I guess the expression on my face shows how furious I am, because he slowly sits down and passes me the crutches.

"I am so mad at you," I sneer through my teeth, lean the crutches on the wall, then turn to take his face in my hands. "How bad is the pain?"

He meets my eyes, but doesn't say anything, just grinds his teeth.

"Shit, baby." I lean in and kiss his forehead. "I'm going to get your painkillers. Two?"

"Make it three."

"Okay. Do you need help getting on the bed?"

"If you take off your clothes and wait for me there, it would be a nice incentive."

"Not tonight, so don't get your hopes up." I brush his cheek and walk into the kitchen.

When I climb into bed with Roman thirty minutes later, he's already knocked out with the triple dose of painkillers. I take the opportunity to watch him. He's usually up before me so I don't get the chance to catch him unguarded. I move a few strands of hair that have fallen over his forehead, and trace the line of his eyebrows, nose, and chin with my finger, admiring his harsh features. God, I was scared shitless tonight. Without a word from him, I was afraid something bad happened.

We'll need to have a serious discussion on that subject tomorrow. I don't think he did it on purpose; I have a feeling Roman simply isn't accustomed to having people being concerned for his well-being. He never talks about his childhood, and I suspect it wasn't an easy one. There's so much I still don't know about him. He rarely shares details regarding his business, and I think he's trying to shield me from that side of his life. But I'm not stupid. In the eyes of the world, my husband is a bad guy. In my eyes, however, he's just Roman. I don't give a fuck about the rest, and that fact scares me a bit, too.

CHAPTER

sixteen

Nina

"W**E COULD'VE STAYED HOME." I GATHER** my skirt and take Roman's hand to exit the car.

"I owed you a dinner."

"We should've gone back home after the restaurant. The club could've been left for some other time."

"I have some business with Pavel here anyway, we won't stay long."

He could have discussed business with Pavel at the house; he's doing this because of me. I just mentioned the club in passing yesterday, saying I had a great time and would like to go again sometime. I didn't expect it to be the following day, damn it. He had to spend the whole day in the wheelchair after that stunt he pulled, and I hate that he's pushing himself on my account. However, there is no discussion with Roman when he gets something into that thick head of his.

We arrive later than we did on our last visit, so the club is already packed. It takes serious maneuvering to get across the first room, even with Ivan leading the way. After we're seated, the waiter brings us drinks. I lean on Roman and turn to tell him something when I notice a tall blond man on the other side of the room. He's standing with his back to me, chatting with a few other guys. I feel Roman's hand come around my waist, and he asks me something. I don't hear the words; my attention is focused on the blond guy. The more I look at him, the shallower my breathing becomes. Someone calls for him. He turns, and it feels like his movements are in slow-motion. Then, his face finally becomes visible. He looks up, our gazes clash, and I stop breathing.

Roman

I feel Nina stiffen next to me. It lasts for a few seconds, and then the hand she placed on my thigh starts shaking.

"Malysh? What's wrong?"

She doesn't react. It's like she hasn't even heard me. She just stares at the crowd. I follow her gaze, trying to see what may have spooked her, but I can't find anything out of ordinary. People are drinking and talking, and nothing stands out except a man near the exit, looking in our direction. I don't like other men looking at my wife, but it's a common occurrence. Nina has an exotic beauty that attracts attention. However, the way this man is staring at her, it's beyond ordinary interest—it's a mix of recognition and malice. He's close to my height, so combined with the horrified way Nina is staring at him, the pieces of the puzzle click into place. Trying hard to control my rage, I take Nina's chin and turn her head to face me.

"Is that the man who hurt you, milaya?"

She looks into my eyes without blinking, her lips pressed into a hard line.

"It's him, isn't it. He'll pay, malysh. He'll pay dearly. I'll make sure of it," I whisper and turn to take my crutches.

Nina grabs my arm. "No. You promised you wouldn't kill anyone because of me."

I never promised such a thing, but her voice is so small and upset, I don't want to distress her further. I'll deal with the bastard later.

"Ivan!" I bark and wait for him to approach. "See that motherfucker? There, below the exit sign. Blond, beard, tall. I want him thrown out of my club, and make sure the bouncers know he's never to be let inside again."

"Yes, Pakhan," he says, and I feel Nina's body relax slightly next to me.

"Good." I put my arm around her back, turn to Ivan, and add in Russian, "Bag him and wait for my call."

Ivan looks at me, and I let him see what I've left unsaid written on my face. He nods, turns, and heads down to the dance floor.

I hold Nina next to me while Ivan and one of the bouncers manhandle the bastard. When I'm sure they're gone, I lead her out of the club. She's silent for the whole trip home, and when we arrive, she goes straight to bed.

"Everything's going to be okay," I whisper in her ear when I join her in bed.

She doesn't answer, just curls into my side, and buries her face in the crook of my neck. After an hour, I finally feel her relax and her breathing evens out. I wait for half an hour more, until I'm sure she's sleeping deeply, then get up and leave the room.

"Where is he?" I ask as soon as Ivan takes the call.

"Pavel has him in his trunk."

"Take him to the basement." I put the phone on the dining room table and leave the suite.

Maneuvering the narrow stairs down to the basement on crutches is a bitch, but I manage, and cross the short hallway that leads into the back room. Inside, the bastard is tied to a chair above the drain, his mouth gagged.

"Remove his shirt," I say to Ivan who's waiting in the corner and turn toward the table by the wall to inspect the assortment of knives and other tools.

"Pakhan? Do you want me to call Mikhail?"

"Nope." I take one of Mikhail's knives and smile. "This one is mine."

Nina

The street in front of me is dark, but I keep running. The sound of my footfalls echoes off the cobblestones lining the ground. Even though I push myself with all my strength, I feel like I'm treading through mud, my legs heavy and slow. A figure of a man comes around the corner, grabs me around my neck, and starts choking me.

I wake with the start and sit up in bed, panting heavily. The lamp in the corner is on, and I find the bed next to me empty. I reach for the phone on the nightstand and check the time. Half past four.

"Roman?" I call out. Nothing but silence answers me.

A sick kind of dread settles in my stomach. I jump out of the bed and run, hoping to find Roman in the kitchen. He isn't there, and I stand in the middle of the room. Did he have some kind of business emergency? But then, my eyes fall on his phone lying on the corner of the dining room table. There's no way he'd leave his phone behind.

I pad down the long hallway on bare feet and open the door to the gym. The lights are out, so I head downstairs to check Roman's office. He's not there, and the whole house is silent. I close his office door, and head toward the main kitchen when my eyes come to the door that leads into the basement. I've never seen anyone going inside, but something urges me to reach for the handle.

The light above the stairs is on, and I hear Roman's voice in the distance below, mixed with some strange sounds of scraping wood. The door must have been soundproofed because I didn't hear anything from the outside. Slowly, I descend the stairs and find myself in an empty room with metal shelves lining the walls. The sounds are louder here. Roman's voice is coming from the direction of the door on the other side that's been left slightly ajar, but I can't decipher what is being said because it's in Russian.

I don't want to see what's happening behind that door, because deep down I know what I'll find inside. But my feet keep leading me forward. I put my palm on the wooden surface and push.

Brian is sitting on a chair in the middle of the tiled floor, his feet and wrists tied to it. On the floor next to his feet, several severed fingers lay scattered in a huge puddle of blood. Roman is standing in front of him, leaning on one crutch with his left hand, and his right is holding a knife that's lodged into Brian's stomach to the hilt. He barks something at him and starts rotating the knife. I stare in horror at the blood pouring from the wound.

A strange, choked sound leaves my lips, and I clutch the doorway next to me as my vision starts to blur. Roman turns abruptly, his eyes widening. He takes a step toward me, and I start retreating, staring at his blood-covered hands. When Roman takes another step in my direction, I turn and run. I don't remember leaving the basement or running up the great stairwell. When I reach the suite, I stumble through my room to the bathroom, locking the door behind me. I take a few shaking breaths, then lunge for the toilet and vomit.

I'm still clutching the sides of the toilet when I hear the knock on the door.

"Leave," I choke out.

"Nina, I—"

"LEAVE!" I scream and then vomit again.

I'm sitting on the floor, next to the toilet, when footsteps approach and Varya's voice calls for me from the other side of the door. It's been an hour or so since I vomited the last time, so I stand up slowly and hunch over the sink. After splashing some cold water onto my face, I unlock the door.

"Dear child," Varya says and reaches for me, but I take a step back.

"I need you to call me a taxi. Please."

"Don't leave. It'll destroy him, Nina. Please, let him explain."

"Taxi," I rasp. "Or I'm going on foot."

Varya looks at me sadly and nods. I see one tear escape and roll down her cheek before she reaches for her phone.

 Roman

There's a knock at the door, but I remain seated in the recliner facing the window and watch the yellow car idling in the driveway.

"Pakhan."

"Yes, Dimitri?"

"There's a taxi waiting out front. Varya said that Nina Petrova is leaving."

"She is."

"Should I stop her?"

I think about it, then shake my head. "No. Send two men to follow her discreetly. Have them call me when she reaches her destination."

"Do you want them to stay there, or come back here?"

"They will stay. I want two men on her constantly. Arrange the shifts. Tell them to make sure they're out of sight."

"Anything else?"

"That's all for now."

A few minutes later, Nina hurries down the steps and gets into the cab. She's wearing jeans and her old hoodie, and is carrying a dog carrier in one hand and a small suitcase in the other. I watch her, waiting for her to turn around and come back inside. She doesn't. The cab leaves.

I grab the crystal bottle of whiskey, pour myself three fingers, and then hurl the bottle across the room, where it shatters against the wall.

CHAPTER
seventeen

Roman

I T'S BEEN FOUR DAYS SINCE NINA LEFT, AND I'M SLOWLY losing my mind. The men who are working as her security detail have been checking in at the end of each shift, updating me on her. It doesn't mean anything other than to let me know she's okay. I want her here, damn it.

At first, I thought she would go to her parents, spend the night, and be back in the morning. But when the guys notified me that she went back to her place, I knew she wouldn't be back the following day. I hoped she'd call—maybe in a day or two. But she hasn't called. I don't want to call her myself until I know she is ready to talk.

I fucked up. I knew that the moment I saw her standing at the basement door, wearing a look of horror and shock on her face, but I didn't expect her to leave.

I can't take waiting anymore, so I grab the phone from my desk and call her. She cuts the call after the second ring without answering. I call again, but all I get back is a clipped response. "We're done, Roman."

She can't do this. I will not allow it. I grab my crutches and stalk toward the door.

"To Nina's place," I bark at Kolya and duck inside the car.

When we reach Nina's building, I take the phone and message her.

I'm outside.

I stare at the phone in my hand, waiting for it to ring. It doesn't. Instead, a message arrives.

WE. ARE. DONE.

LEAVE.

What the fuck am I supposed do with this? Should I go up, break down her door, and make her listen to me? And what would I say? There's no way to take back what's been done.

I stay in the car in front of her building. Well into the night, I finally tell Kolya to take me home. It's too soon. I'll give her a few more days to cool down. Then we'll speak.

Two days later, a package arrives. It's a big rectangular thing wrapped in brown paper, and it has my name written in Nina's messy handwriting. I place it on my desk, trace the letters she wrote with my finger, and start tearing the paper.

It's a painting.

A naked woman is kneeling in the middle of a field of debris and ashes, her back arched backward, arms slightly raised toward the stormy sky above. Her black hair is flowing in the wind, part of it covering her face. A long black spear is lodged in the middle of her chest, and a thick layer of red paint is trailing from the wound down her nude body. On the other end of the spear, a lone vulture is perched, as if waiting.

The self-portrait she promised me.

I get up and gaze at the lawn beyond the window until the sun sets, then go back to the desk. Placing my elbows on the wooden surface I bury my hands in my hair and stare at the painting, noticing the small details I missed the first time. The way the veins in the woman's neck are standing out as if she's straining. Red tears falling down her cheeks. Black cracks on the skin of her chest where the spear pierced it—thicker around the wound and getting thinner as they radiate away, like her body itself started breaking apart.

She's not coming back.

Nina

I SIT DOWN AT THE DINING TABLE, PLACE THE MANILA folder on the surface in front of me and just look at it. Twenty minutes pass before I gather the courage to open the folder and take out the papers. I grab a pen from the cup, place its point at the beginning of the dotted line in the bottom left corner and start signing my name. My vision blurs and tears pour from my eyes, falling onto the paper below and smearing the ink. Shit.

I crumple the ruined document, take another copy from the folder and start over. Somewhere on the third page, my hand starts shaking, but I keep signing. At the fifth one, I break down and start sobbing. I can't even see the damn paper anymore, so I get up and leave the kitchen to calm down. It takes me more than two hours to sign all three copies of the divorce papers. Then, I seal them into a big envelope, write Roman's address, and call the courier.

Roman

"This just arrived." Varya hands me a big white envelope. "It's from Nina."

I tear the side of the envelope, take out a folder with a set of papers inside, and place it on my desk without opening it.

"This better not be what I think it is," I sneer through clenched teeth as I open the folder and stare at the first document.

"Roman? What's going on?" Varya asks and rounds the table to stand next to me.

"She wants a divorce." I grab the desk and launch the damn thing toward the center of the room where it lands upside down, sending the laptop and papers flying. "She is not getting the fucking divorce!" I yell.

Nina

The papers come back two days later. Standing at the door, I tear the envelope, take the papers out and stare at the line in the right corner where Roman's name is printed. Above it, on the dotted line where his signature should be, a big "No" is written in red ink. I turn the page. The same big red "No" on this one. And on the next. And the next.

"Damn you, Roman."

I grab my phone and call my lawyer. "I need more copies of the divorce papers."

I send the papers again the same day. They come back a day later, but instead of his signature, every bottom right corner is burned off.

Next time I receive the envelope back, there are no papers inside. Instead, there's a bunch of white ashes.

I want to scream and laugh at the same time, but I end up crying again. By the next morning, I decide that enough is enough, grab my phone and call him. He answers on the first ring.

"Nina. You've received my answer, I take it."

Just hearing his voice makes me want to weep, but I steel myself and try my best to sound normal. "I need you to sign the divorce papers."

"No."

"Roman, please."

"I am not giving you a fucking divorce!" he yells into the phone. "You left me, and that was your choice. This is mine."

"Do you want to know what I want Roman? Do you even care?"

He sighs. "What do you want, Nina?"

"I want at least a remotely normal life, Roman. I want someone who won't decide to play God and serve his own justice, killing off people he doesn't like. I don't want to witness that. Brian was a bastard, but I didn't want him killed because of me. I never wanted that on my conscience. I asked you and begged you to leave it be. And you gutted him like a pig. I still have nightmares about that night, Roman."

I take a deep breath before I continue.

"I can't live in your world, Roman, where I'm fucking terrified every time you go to arrange some deal or whatever. I thought I could, but I can't. Do you have any idea what it did to me, to sit at the window the whole night while you were out on business? I imagined you in a ditch somewhere and waited for them bring you back either shot or dead! But most of all, I can't live with the possibility that someday you'll decide to gut someone else just because he looked at me in a funny way, or whatever. I can't! It's tearing me apart from the inside out. What you did to Brian, it's eating me up. This guilt, knowing that someone is dead because of me. I can't eat. I can't sleep. I keep seeing his body covered in blood, pieces of his fingers on the floor. God, Roman . . . I can't unsee all that blood on your hands."

I'm sobbing so hard at the end that I'm not sure if he understood even half of what I said.

"Do you understand, Roman?"

There is only silence on the other side of the line, and I start to wonder if he cut the connection when I finally hear his voice.

"Yes. I understand," he says, and the line goes dead.

A day later, another envelope arrives. I open it and go through the papers. He signed. I look at his signature, and it hurts so damn much that, at first, I don't even see the note penned at the top of the page.

"If you ever need me, you know my number. If you don't want to have anything to do with me, call Maxim or Dimitri. I've instructed them that, in case you ever call, they are to do what you ask, and not share it with me. Please, call Varya from time to time. She misses you. Take care, malysh."

I clutch the note to my chest as my heart breaks into a million little pieces.

CHAPTER
nineteen

Two weeks later

I LEAN BACK AND REGARD MAXIM AS HE APPROACHES my desk.

"I'm listening," I say.

"The next shipment is set to arrive tomorrow night."

"How many crates?"

"Eleven. That's the best we could do on short notice."

"Make sure you check every gun. I don't want mishaps on Saturday. Italians don't suspect anything?"

"No."

"Good. Make sure you rotate the men frequently for the next few days. What's the assault plan?"

"Two teams. Six foot soldiers each. Dimitri and Anton will be going with the first team. Mikhail and Yuri with the second."

"Leave Mikhail out." I shake my head. "I don't want to risk him getting shot, Lena needs him. Send Sergei instead."

"I don't think it's a good idea. Sergei's behavior became even more erratic recently. He won't follow Yuri's orders."

"Of course, he won't." I curse and throw the document I've been reading. "I'll go with Sergei. Yuri can't shoot worth a damn anyway."

Maxim stares at me as if I've gone mad. Maybe I have. "Over my dead body, Roman."

"It's not open for a discussion. I'm the only one who can make sure Sergei behaves."

He regards me with his jaw set in hard line, takes off his glasses and angrily points them at me. "You can't fucking walk."

"Maybe I can't walk, but other than Sergei, I'm still Bratva's best shooter."

"I won't allow it, Roman. It's suicide."

"Oh? Then let's just give a mentally unstable person a gun and a bunch of explosives, and send him on the field without supervision? Sergei is capable of annihilating a whole city block in under an hour."

"Well, we won't send Sergei then. You pulled him from field duty for a reason."

"This is a special occasion. With supervision, having Sergei in the field is like having a one-man assault battalion. I need either Mikhail or Sergei on Saturday. And Mikhail is staying out of it."

Maxim doesn't comment, only shakes his head and squeezes his temples.

"You never saw Sergei in the field." I lean back in my chair as a serene smile spreads over my face. "It's a thing of beauty. Do you know he once cleared an enemy warehouse all by himself? Fourteen people. And he only got shot once."

"It's no wonder you two are blood-related," Maxim sighs. "You're both completely insane."

"Well, that's settled then." I lean forward to close the laptop. "What about her?"

"She's having an exhibit next month. Ivan saw the poster."

"Just the showing, or a sales exhibit?"

"I'll check."

"If it's sales, call the gallery in advance and buy everything." I look up. "Anonymously. Anything else?"

I notice him tense and look to the side.

"Anything else, Maxim?"

"She's changed her hair."

"Did she cut it?"

"No. Just dyed it."

"Blonde?"

"No. It . . . it's purple."

She dyed her hair purple. I can't help but smile a little.

"That's all, Maxim."

Nina

One month later

DIFFERENT SHADES OF BLACK AND GRAY, AND nothing else. I take some of the yellow paint on my brush and try adding a few strokes over the dark shapes on my canvas, but it only ends up smeared with the previous layer of black. It kind of reflects my state of mind the last few weeks. Shades of black, and every single attempt to add a little bit of color ends up as a fluke. I shouldn't have returned Brando. Maybe with him here I wouldn't feel so alone.

I leave the canvas to dry and go to the bathroom. The previous layers should dry by tomorrow evening, and I'll try again. I wonder when I'll be able to process anything other than shades of gray. It certainly won't be tomorrow.

Three tubes of hair dye lay scattered next to the sink. I've already tried purple, and it lasted for two weeks before it washed out. How fitting. I reach for the second tube. Maybe the blue will last longer.

It takes me two hours to finish with my hair and take a shower, and it's almost six a.m. when I finally go into my bedroom. The sun is already started rising, so I pull the heavy drapes over the window and climb into bed. I still can't sleep during the night, so I switched and started going to bed early in the morning and working through the night instead. The moment I'd close my eyes I'd see Roman turning the knife again, his hands covered in blood. That scene was much easier to deal with during the day.

That phase passed after a month, and now the only thing I see in my dreams is Roman. Unfortunately, nothing makes it easier to deal with this new vision, day or night. Sometimes, when I find it especially hard to sleep, I close my eyes and pretend that he's next to me.

Maybe I should leave, pack a bag and catch the first train to wherever, switch at a random point, until I'm somewhere far away. I could find a job on a farm or something, cleaning horse shit, and painting in my free time. Or I could start using horse shit instead of paint. Start a new artistic wave. Yeah, I'll consider that.

Roman

Maxim enters my kitchen and stands by the island, his hands clasped behind his back. He watches the doc work on my arm.

"Italians rigged one of our warehouses," he says.

"The damage?"

"Just the building, nothing that can't be repaired."

"Anyone hurt?"

"It was one of the empty warehouses, so there wasn't any security detail allocated there."

Leave it to the Italians to burn an empty warehouse. Idiots. "Make sure you double the men on the ones holding products."

"Already done."

I thank the doc, stand up, and go toward the window overlooking the patio. "What has she been doing?"

"She's changed her hair again. It's blue now."

"Any . . . men?"

"No one, as far as we could see."

"When a man enters the picture, and it will happen eventually, make sure I never find out, Maxim."

CHAPTER
Twenty-one

Roman

One month later

"I VAN CALLED." I HEAR MAXIM'S VOICE IN MY earpiece. "Two cars just passed them, and they're coming your way. Get the fuck out of there."

I curse. "Sergei is still inside," I say, check my gun, and focus my gaze on the back of the Italians' warehouse.

"They'll be there in less than five minutes, Roman."

"I'm not leaving him."

"I told you to take more men with you! Damn it, Roman, you never listen."

"There should've only been two security guys. Maybe someone tipped them off. We're leaving as soon as Sergei's out."

I turn to Anton, who's sitting in the driver's seat, and nod toward the back door on the far side of the warehouse, fifty or so feet away. "The moment you see Sergei, floor it. We're going to have company."

Two minutes later, I hear the cars approaching from the right, and the next moment, the door at the back of the warehouse opens and Sergei runs out.

"Go!" I bark.

Anton starts the car, speeding toward Sergei. I open the window, aim at one of the vehicles approaching from the side road and start shooting. The first car swerves, the driver probably losing control after a bullet hits a tire, and smashes into a tree. The second car passes it and speeds toward us. I shoot twice more, and Anton suddenly hits the break. There's a sound of a door opening, and Sergei jumps in.

"You two are partying without me," he says and laughs. Maniac.

"Drive!" I shout to Anton, change the magazine, and resume shooting at the Italians who have stopped twenty feet from us and are trying to get out of their vehicle. I manage to hit both front tires before our car lurches forward.

"Blast them," I call over my shoulder, my eyes still on the Italians' car.

"Sure." I hear Sergei say from behind me. A second later, I hear the explosion.

I look at the rearview mirror and see the west part of the warehouse collapsing.

"Let Maxim know we're out," I tell Anton, then turn to Sergei. "Were there any problems?"

"Other than you taking away most of my stuff, no."

"I wanted only their building destroyed. You brought enough explosive to blow up half a continent." I shake my head. Maxim was right. He is completely unstable.

Nina

I open the door and stare at my mother. "What are you doing here?"

"You haven't been answering your phone for weeks. I was worried."

I move to the side to let her in, close the door, and walk into my living room. "I messaged you yesterday."

"Yeah, your 'I'm okay, stop calling' didn't convince me. How are you feeling?"

"Like a train wreck." I shrug, take the brush, and resume working on my painting.

"You look awful, Nina."

"Thanks, Mom."

From the corner of my eye, I see her come into the room and slowly turn around, looking at the paintings I've lined along the walls.

"You usually add some bright color. All of those are plain gray and black?" she asks.

"How would you know that? You were never interested in my art."

She doesn't reply but comes to stand next to me and watches me paint for a few moments. "I've got the one with the girl in a green dress. We've hung it in the living room."

My brush on the canvas goes still. "I thought that one was sold with the others to an anonymous buyer. Did they return them?"

"No. He let me have it."

I look up at her. "He?"

"Your husband. He's the one who bought the paintings."

I take a deep breath and turn back toward my canvas. "He's not my husband anymore."

I try to resume my work, but my hand holding the brush is trembling, so I put the brush down, and stare at the unfinished black shape in front of me. My mother takes me by the shoulder and turns me toward her.

"What happened between you two, honey? I thought you would be staying together."

"I walked in on him gutting Brian," I say. "After he cut off most of his fingers."

"He killed him?"

"Yes."

She's silent for a moment, and then she shakes her head. "He loves you."

I feel the tears start gathering in my eyes. "Yes, he does. But sometimes love is not enough."

"You knew who he was, Nina, and still, you fell in love with him. Can't you forgive him?"

"He would do it again, Mom. I can't live with another death on my conscience. This one is already too much. Does that make me a hypocrite? That it never bothered me what he did or who he killed before?"

"It's how his world works. But not yours."

I turn toward the canvas and pick up my brush again. "I have to finish this one by tomorrow."

"Okay, honey. I'll let you work." She reaches out with her hand and brushes the back of my palm lightly. "Please answer when I call."

I hear my mom's footsteps moving away, then stop. I turn and see her standing in the doorway, her head slightly bent.

"I was wrong about your husband," she says, then lifts her head and our gazes connect. There's a strange look on her face. I am completely confused by her words, and this whole visit in general.

"Your father would never kill a man because of me, you know."

"Well, that's a good thing, Mom."

"No, honey. It isn't," she says and leaves the apartment.

Nina

One week later

MY PHONE STARTS RINGING ON THE NIGHTSTAND, but I ignore it and put a pillow over my head. The ringing stops, just to start again a minute later. I groan, reach for the damn thing, and answer without looking who's calling.

"Did I wake you up, child?"

I sit up in the bed, instantly awake. "Varya?"

"I need to talk to you. Can I drop by?"

"Sure, I'll text you the address."

"I'll be there in an hour then."

"Varya, what's happening? Is . . . is he okay?"

"Yes. For now, at least. We'll talk when I get there."

A bad feeling forms in my chest while I stare at my phone. Something is wrong, I know it. I rush into the bathroom to shower and change. I'm collecting the brushes and discarded sketches littering the floor in my living room when I hear the doorbell.

"What the fuck has he done now?" I ask the moment Varya comes inside.

"I like the hair, kukolka. Green looks good on you." She kisses me and smiles, but it doesn't reach her eyes. "Let's sit."

I lead her into the kitchen, pour us two cups of coffee, and sit down in the chair opposite Varya. She slides the cup toward herself and holds it in her hands, looking at the liquid inside. "Can you please come back?"

Her question stuns me, and for a second, I stare at her speechlessly. "I'm not coming back. We divorced three months ago; you know that."

"Roman started a war with the Italians. He did it on purpose. They've been playing cat and mouse for months now, attacking each other's shipments, blowing up warehouses."

"Dear God. What the hell was he thinking?"

"He wasn't. I think he wanted a distraction, and the Italians were a convenient choice."

"A hell of a distraction. Has he gone mad?"

"Maybe." She shrugs and takes a sip of her coffee. "I was there when he signed the divorce papers, you know. I think, up until that point, he believed you'd come back eventually. But after signing those papers . . . he just snapped. Two weeks later he sent the guys to intercept one of the Italians' shipments. And he went with them."

"He did *what*?"

"He said it was because he needed to keep an eye on Sergei, and I assumed it was a onetime thing. It wasn't."

"I thought a pakhan is supposed to handle the

organization, manage business deals or whatever, not play foot soldier."

"He doesn't seem to care, child. Do you know how big a deal it is in our world if a soldier manages to kill a pakhan? The one who does that becomes a hero among his peers. When it's just the soldiers on the field, it's business as usual, but with a pakhan there, he becomes the primary target."

"Varya, I . . . I don't know what you expect me to do. Call him and ask him to stop acting like an idiot?"

"I need you to come back. With you there, he won't be so reckless. He wouldn't want you to worry."

"He's a grown man, Varya. He doesn't need me to act as his off switch."

"Roman loves you, Nina. I don't think you know how much."

"A man died because of me. I told Roman I can't live with that, and he killed him anyway. If he truly loved me, he would have never done that to me."

"Do you know how Roman became a pakhan, child?" Varya asks, and I shake my head. "Let me tell you that story. It might help you understand things better."

She looks down at her cup and starts stirring the liquid with a spoon.

"Roman's mother married his father when she was only eighteen. Lev was twenty years older than her, and he was a really bad man, kukolka. I came into that house with Nastya. I had known her since she was a baby, and I hated seeing Lev mistreating her from the moment she arrived. He beat her, even while she was pregnant with Roman. When Roman was five, he started confronting his father on purpose so Lev would take out his anger on him instead of

Nastya. It worked for a few months. Until it didn't. A few days before Roman's sixth birthday, Lev hit Nastya so hard that she fell down the stairs. Roman watched."

"He killed her?"

"Yes. Broken neck. I took over taking care of Roman then. Lev married again a few years later, but Marina managed to run away. I'm not sure what happened to her, but we never heard anything about her afterward."

"You think he killed her, too?"

"Probably. When Roman grew up, I started working as a housekeeper and tried my best to keep myself as far away as possible from the pakhan. I handled the staff and didn't have any reason to cross Lev's path. Until he called for me one day. When I came into the library, he grabbed me around my neck and slammed me into the wall, choking me. He was mad because the maid didn't change the sheets that morning as he requested. When Roman came in, I was half passed out already. Roman killed him, and if he didn't, Lev would have choked me to death."

I look up at Varya, who is looking pointedly at the hand I raised at some point and unconsciously placed on my neck.

"We all have some kind of trigger, child. Roman saw that man as a threat to you, and he neutralized it. I'm not saying he did the right thing. I'm just trying to make you understand. He knows now that what he did hurt you, and believe me when I say he'd never do anything intentionally that could inflict any kind of pain on you. He's madly in love with you, and I think when you left, it broke something in him. He doesn't care about anything anymore. I think he's doing all those reckless things on purpose. He . . . he got shot last month."

"What?" I whisper, and the tears I've been keeping at bay burst out.

"In his upper arm. He was lucky—it just went through, nothing serious. This time. Please, at least talk to him. He's going to get himself killed, Nina. It's just a matter of time."

"Oh, I'll talk to him." I stand up from the table and hurry to grab my jacket and wallet, brushing my tears away with the sleeve of my shirt along the way. "I'll call us a taxi."

"Vova can take us. I think it's his shift," Varya says casually.

"He's somewhere in the neighborhood?"

"You could say that. He's across the street."

I raise my head to look at her, then go to the window and look outside. Like she said, there's a nondescript car sitting there. "He put a tail on me?"

"He put a security detail on you. They've been there for months."

"I'm going to kill him."

When we exit the building, I march right across the street toward the car and knock on the window. Vova's head snaps up, and he stares at me with wide eyes and quickly lowers the window.

"Nina Petrova?"

I grind my teeth but don't correct him, only motion with my head to Varya who is approaching.

"We need a ride."

"Of course." He unlocks the door, and we get in the back. "Where do you need to go?"

"I'm paying Pakhan a visit," I say and lean back into the seat.

It takes us close to an hour to reach the house. The moment the car stops in the driveway, I get out and rush up the stone steps toward the main door. The security guy, who is standing guard, looks at me with surprise, then nods and opens the door for me.

"Where is he, Kolya?"

"I believe Pakhan is in his office," he says.

I rush across the hall and turn left toward the west wing corridor leading to Roman's office. The closer I get to his door, the more my bravado leaks out of me. By the time I reach the door, I'm a bundle of nerves and anxiety. I'm going to see him again after all this time, and I'm both excited and scared. I want to go inside, but at the same time, I want to turn around and bolt. There's no going back now—it's too late.

Placing my hand on the handle, I take a deep breath, school my features into an expressionless mask, and enter without knocking.

Roman is sitting behind his desk, looking between papers in his hands and the laptop screen. I let the door behind me close, lean my back onto it, and watch him for a few seconds. God, I've missed him so much that just looking at him hurts.

"I hear you got yourself shot," I say, and I'm amazed how casual I manage to sound—not a tremor in my voice, but a hurricane rages inside.

Roman's head snaps up, his gaze colliding with mine, and

he stares me down with such force that if I didn't have the door behind me, I would have stumbled backward. So much is going on in his eyes, different emotions flashing and being replaced with others so quickly, I can't catch all of them. There is surprise, but it's mixed with hurt and so much rage that I can't help but flinch.

"And that concerns you how, Nina?" Quiet, angry words—each one piercing my already shredded heart. He hates me.

"I just wanted to make sure you're okay."

He leans back in his chair and crosses his arms in front of him. "Why?"

Why? Such a simple question. And so many answers. Because I was afraid for him. Because I missed him and wanted to see him even if only for a minute. Because I love him. But instead of answering, I stand there and try to control my breathing because, suddenly, it feels like there's not enough air in the room.

Roman stands up, reaches for the cane leaning on the desk, and walks toward me. He is leaning on his cane quite heavily, but his steps are sure and rather quick. One tear escapes from the corner of my eye. He did it; I knew he would.

He comes to stand in front of me and raises his hand to place it on the door next to my head, caging me in. He lowers his head so that our faces are only inches apart.

"I asked you a question. I need an answer, malysh."

The dam bursts upon me hearing his endearment, and the tears flow freely down my face. My lower lip starts quivering so I bite it and slowly raise my hands to his face. They're trembling. I hesitate for a second, then place my palms on his cheeks.

"You. Left. Me," he whispers, and then bangs the door with his palm. "You fucking left me!"

"I know."

Rage. So much rage in his eyes as he looks down at me, his jaw set in a hard line.

"I'm sorry for hurting you," he whispers. "I wish I could turn back time and do things differently. I can't, and that's a fact. But I am not sorry for killing that bastard. That's another fact for you. I'll ask again. Why do you care if I was shot?"

I can't make myself look away from his eyes. He's not sorry for what he did. Can I live with that?

Roman clenches his jaw, reaches with his hand, and buries it in the hair at the back of my head. "Answer me, damn it!"

"Because I love you, Roman!" I press my palms onto his cheeks and shake his stubborn head. "I love you. I can't bear the thought of you getting hurt. You will end this fucking war you've started, you hear me? I don't care how you do it, but end it, or so help me God, I'm going to kill you myself."

He doesn't say anything for a few moments, staring into my eyes with his fingers clutching the back of my head.

"Marry me," he says, "and I'll stop the war."

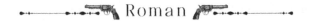

Roman

Nina's eyes go wide at my proposition. She's probably wondering if I'm serious, and you bet I am. No matter the means, I'm getting her back.

"You're blackmailing me into marrying you. Again."

It's not a question, but I decide to clarify anyway. "Yes, I am."

Her eyes stare into mine, and I watch them closely. They're red at the edges, and the tears are still flowing. I don't think she even notices she's still crying, and I yearn to brush them away with my hand. This will be the last time she cries because of me. I vow it to myself.

I need her to say yes. There is no way I can go through one more night without my wildcat curled into my side. She took my black heart with her the day she left, and if she says no, she can keep it. I'm ruined for anyone else anyway.

"Jesus, Roman," she sighs and presses the heels of her palms over her eyes.

I stare at her hands, which are smeared with black paint, and a tiny flame of hope rises in my chest. "You didn't take off the rings."

"I couldn't." She lowers her hands and sniffs.

Okay. We're getting somewhere. I reach for her hand and take off the rings from her finger. They come off too easily. She's lost weight. I'm going to strangle her.

"Give those back!" she yelps and grabs for my hand, but I move it behind my back.

"I will. Just give me a few seconds," I say, and gripping the cane, I slowly start lowering my left knee toward the floor.

Nina stares at me, her eyes wide. She's crying again. "Shit, baby. Don't do that."

I ignore the screaming pain in my right leg and lower my left knee a bit more. It's not the exact pose I envisioned, but it's the closest to getting on one knee I can manage. I raise the rings in front of her.

"Will you marry me, malysh?"

She whimpers and exhales, tears still streaming down her face, then grabs the front of my shirt and pulls me up. It takes me a few seconds to straighten, and when I do, she raises her hand between us.

"You're not getting away with the cheap version this time, Roman." She sniffs. "I want a dress, big and fluffy and sparkling. I want a ton of flowers, an orchestra playing fancy music, and of course—"

I feel my lips curl up in a smile. I am so fucking in love with my crazy little wife.

"I love you," I whisper, slide the rings onto her finger, then grab her face and kiss her.

I trace my palm down Nina's back, then lower it to squeeze her ass, and retrace the path up all the way to the back of her head where my fingers get stuck in tangled dark green strands. "Will this wash off?"

Nina lifts her head from my chest and looks at the strand of hair between my fingers. "Not a fan of green?"

"Not really. But if you like it, I'm okay with it. It's awful, though."

"It'll wash off in a week or so. I hate it too." She shrugs and places her head down again, just over my heart. "How will you stop the war with the Italians?"

"The usual way. Someone is going to get married to a sweet and docile Italian girl."

"How romantic. And who will be the lucky groom?"

"I haven't decided yet. Probably Kostya."

220

"I'm sure he'll be thrilled." She yawns and closes her eyes. "How's the physical therapy been going?"

"I finished it two weeks ago. Warren said we've reached the maximum of what could be achieved, so there's no need for it anymore."

"I'm glad. I know how much you hated those sessions. You're sexy with the cane, just like I predicted." She smiles sleepily.

I lift a few tangled strands of hair from her face, then look to the side of the bed where my crutches are leaning on the wall. I don't think she noticed them when we came in, since we were preoccupied with removing our clothes on the way to the bed. She'd find out in the morning anyway, but I prefer to tell her right away and be done with it.

"Nina . . . I have to tell you something."

"Mhm . . . can it wait till the morning?"

"No."

Her head snaps up immediately, her eyes staring me down. "What did you do?"

"I didn't do anything. It's just something I need you to know."

"Oh, God . . ." she groans, "Just tell me what the fuck you did."

My beautiful little flower is watching me, her eyes wide. I hate that I have to tell her. I hate it so much it makes me sick.

"I'm still using the crutches, Nina. My knee is still stiff in the mornings, and I can't walk without them for the first hour or so." I grit my teeth and continue, "I sometimes need them in the evenings, too."

She's just watching me, her eyes staring into mine. I need her to say something. Anything.

"And?" she asks finally.

"And what? That's it," I say.

Her eyes widen even more.

"Holy fuck, Roman, don't scare me like that." She hits me on the chest with her palm. "I thought you were going to tell me something important, like how you offed Igor while I was away. Christ, baby."

I stare at her. Not the reaction I expected. Disappointment, yes. Or at least some displeasure when she realized she'll end up tied to a disabled man for the rest of her life. Isn't that important? Maybe she thinks it's only temporary.

"Nina, you don't understand. It won't get any better than this for me. I'm sorry, malysh."

She leans forward until her forehead touches mine and places her palms on either side of my face. "Yes, you already told me. I also saw your crutches and deduced as much myself, baby. And I couldn't care less." She places a kiss on my lips. "So, you didn't kill anyone while I was away?"

I decide to plead the Fifth, and wisely keep my mouth shut.

"Roman?" She narrows her eyes at me.

I sigh. "I offed Tanush, okay?"

"I knew it. I . . ." She shakes her head.

"He was the one who set up the bomb with Leonid."

Nina regards me, scrunches her nose, then nods. "He deserved it." She says and resumes her position on my chest. "Just please don't kill anyone else because of me."

I listen until her breathing evens out. When I'm sure she's sleeping soundly, I take her small hand from my chest and place a kiss on the tips of her fingers.

"I will be killing anyone who dares to hurt you," I whisper. "I'll just make sure you don't find out next time."

epilogue

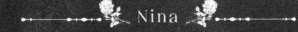

Nina

Two months later

"YOU ARE NOT COMING WITH ME TO BUY THE wedding dress, Roman." I glare at him from the other side of the kitchen, my hands on my hips.

"I'll be outside the changing room. I won't look, but I *will* be there."

"No," I say.

"Yes."

"This is ridiculous."

"There is nothing ridiculous about my fear for your safety. I still can't forget the day when the bastard Leonid hired tried to kill you. You have no idea what that one hour of not knowing if you were hurt or dead did to me. I will not go through that again."

He comes in front of me, scoops me up with his arm

around my waist, and deposits me on the counter. It has become my favorite spot.

"Show off." I reach out and squeeze his rock-hard biceps.

"You love when I do that," he says and stands between my legs. "And it saves me from straining my neck."

I feel his hand at the back of my knee, then traveling up along my thigh to my panties. He places his cane onto the counter, and then his other hand slides under my skirt.

"I'll be late for the fitting."

"They will wait," he whispers in my ear, and suddenly I hear the fabric of my panties tear. "I'll have to find the architect who calculated the height of this counter . . ." He reaches for his belt, unclasps it, and starts unbuttoning his pants. "And I'll tip them well."

"How well?" I smile, hook my legs around his waist, and take a hold of the counter edge.

"Extremely." He grabs my butt cheeks and buries himself in me with one thrust.

"Roman," I say an hour later. "I want to try again."

His hand stills on my back. "No."

We've been trying to get over my fears and it seems we're getting somewhere. Having him hold my wrists doesn't trigger me anymore. We tried that first. However, when we tried with me lying on my back, we hit a dead-end. Whenever Roman tried to lie above me, even without actually pinning me with his body, I'd freak out. It was tearing me apart from the inside. I wanted to feel his body covering mine so much, but my mind always processed the situation the wrong way. I don't know what to do to make my fucked-up brain "un-fuck" itself.

I raise my head and look him in the eyes. "Please?"

Roman's hand cups my face, his gaze burning into mine, and I see it in his eyes. It's bothering him, too.

"Do you have any idea what it does to me, feeling you go still with fear beneath me, watching the panic in your eyes? It guts me every time. Please don't ask me to keep hurting you. I can't bear it."

"Just one more try," I beg, working to keep the tears from falling. I love him so much, why can't my stupid brain understand that he'd never do me harm?

Roman sighs and kisses my forehead. "Okay."

I turn to lie on my back, take his hand and place it on my stomach where he starts caressing my skin. Carefully, Roman moves his right leg over mine, and gets closer until his chest and stomach are plastered to my side.

"All good?" he whispers, and I nod.

Slowly, he rises on his elbow and places his other hand on my other side. I take a deep breath and watch him as he moves to a position above me, supporting his weight on his elbows. My breathing quickens and I see him go still. He'll pull away. I see it on his face. No. I will not let this absurd fear rule me anymore.

I reach with my hand, noting the way my fingers are trembling, and place it on his cheek. "I need you to talk to me, baby." I have to make my brain understand it's Roman.

"I love you, milaya. So, so much," he whispers without breaking our eye contact. "I think I fell in love with you that first time we met. You were so badass, in that black emo outfit and nose ring, standing in front of me so composed and oh so angry."

My breathing is still faster than normal, and my hand is still trembling, and I feel this need to run away, but I grind my teeth and focus on Roman's voice.

"You bewitched me, my little flower. That night, at the party where we supposedly met, I wanted to kiss you the moment you told me you were not a poodle."

I place my other hand on his chest, feeling his heartbeat under my palm. My labored breathing slows a little bit.

"Do you believe in love at first sight, malysh?" he says and his head lowers a few inches. "I always thought it utter nonsense. I was wrong. So wrong."

His head dips even lower until his nose is almost touching mine, those devious eyes staring into my own.

"I love you so much, I would burn the fucking world for you." Our lips almost touch. "You created a monster, Nina, because there is nothing I wouldn't do. You only need to ask."

My hands almost stop shaking, and my breathing is settling back to normal. Slowly, I wrap my arms around his neck and pull him so those last few inches close, until his mouth finally touches mine.

"Please don't burn anything today, baby," I say into his lips.

I feel his mouth widen and see the corners of his eyes crinkle. "I'll think about it," he whispers and kisses me.

There is a slight weight pressing on my chest. Roman is still supporting himself on his elbows but his front is almost plastered to mine. I have a moment of panic when I register his body's position, but then my brain focuses on his lips, and my muscles relax. God, this man can kiss.

"More, baby," I mumble into his lips, and he allows a bit more of his weight to rest on me.

"Good?"

Not just good. Perfect. And now the hardest part. "Hand on my neck, Roman."

"Nina."

"Please."

His right hand slowly moves over my chest, then higher, until his palm reaches my neck. My breath catches. My hands go still on his shoulders, and I shut my eyes.

"It's just me." I hear his voice whispering in my ear as his fingers caress the skin on my neck. "I will never do you any harm. I'd rather chop off my own hand. Please come back to me. You know what a wreck I am without you, malysh."

A tear escapes when I open my eyes and look at him—my big bad husband, who's watching me with concern.

"I love you so fucking much, it's unhealthy," I say, then slam my mouth onto his and wrap my legs around his waist.

Roman enters me slowly, he's still afraid that I might flip out, but I know I won't. I was never afraid that he'd hurt me, and it looks like my fucked-up brain finally got the memo. I move my lips to his ear.

"I want you to fuck me senseless, Roman," I utter. "And if I can walk afterward, you *will* face consequences."

He growls, slowly slides out of me, then buries himself again, making me moan. I never thought I would enjoy the feel of a huge male body weighing me down so much. Roman's hand trails over my breast and stomach until he reaches the place where our bodies are joined. Pressing my clit, his masterful fingers circle, tease. I grab onto his shoulders, panting, as he continues to destroy my pussy and me, sliding in and out as my heartbeat skyrockets.

"Harder," I choke out and arch my back.

Roman's hand leaves my pussy and travels down my thigh, then, wrapping his fingers around my knee, he pulls my leg up and over his shoulder. When he thrusts into me again, I gasp. The sensation of his cock filling me so completely scrambles my brain. He bends his head to place a kiss on my lips, then pounds into me so hard I have to use the headboard to brace myself. The bed under me rocks to the tempo of his thrusts, and a whimper leaves my lips. My muscles spasm, but he keeps pushing my body harder and harder until I come with a scream.

Roman

I love when she plays with my hair. Of course, I would never admit it. It's not something that would be considered pakhanish, as Nina likes to say.

"I think I'll have to reschedule the fitting," she says and continues running her fingers through my hair. "We're three hours late, and I'm sure they are fully booked up. There's no way they'll be able to squeeze me in."

"Of course, they will." I crack one eyelid open and look at her. "No one says no to my wife."

"Well, technically, I'm not your wife, yet. Or should I say anymore-yet?" Her hand stills and I growl with displeasure. "I guess we're between marriages. This situation is bizarre."

"We'll correct it soon enough." I shrug and close my eyes again.

"Roman?"

"Mhm?"

"I have some news to share. I don't know how you'll react, but please don't freak out. Do you promise not to freak out?"

"Nina, milaya, I never freak out. I am an extremely composed person. You know that. What is it?"

I feel her hair tingling my shoulder as she bends and whispers in my ear. "I'm pregnant."

My eyes snap open. It feels like I've been hit with a train, and there is a weight pressing on my chest, making it difficult to breathe. I grab her around her back and plaster her body to mine, tucking her head under my chin. "Are you sure? Please tell me you're sure."

"I'm sure. I did a test this morning because I've been vomiting up breakfast for a week or so. And my boobs are killing me, as well. I haven't been on the pill since I came back."

I shut my eyes and hold her for a few moments, processing.

"I'm not letting you out of my sight," I whisper in her ear. "You are not to leave the house without me. I'm telling the maids to transfer my things from the office. I'll be working from the living room from now on."

"Roman! Are you fucking insane?"

"I might be. I am crazy with happiness and fucking terrified at the same time. And you do not want to agitate a crazy person, Nina. Believe that."

"What the hell happened to that extremely composed man you claimed to be?"

"Gone." I kiss the crown of her head . "We're canceling the fitting and going to a doctor for a checkup right away."

"I knew you'd freak out," she sighs into my neck. "God, I hope it will be a boy."

"Why?" I ask. "I would love to have a girl."

"She'll never have a boyfriend with your crazy self around, Roman."

"Of course, she will. When she's fifty." I move my hand between our bodies to place my palm over Nina's stomach. "I love you so much."

"I love you too, my dangerous kotik."

The  End

Dear reader,

Thanks so much for reading! I hope you'll consider leaving a review and letting the other readers know what you thought of *Painted Scars*. Reviews help authors find new readers, and help other readers find new books to love!

NEXT IN THE SERIES

PERFECTLY IMPERFECT SERIES
Mikhail & Bianca

A marriage
between the two sides.

The most beautiful woman
of the Italian mafia,

And the Bratva's
most feared monster.

BROKEN
whispers
NEVA ALTAJ

ABOUT THE
author

Neva Altaj writes steamy contemporary mafia romance about damaged antiheroes and strong heroines who fall for them. She has a soft spot for crazy jealous, possessive alphas who are willing to burn the world to the ground for their woman. Her stories are full of heat and unexpected turns, and a happily-ever-after is guaranteed every time.

Neva loves to hear from her readers,
so feel free to reach out:

Website: www.neva-altaj.com

Facebook: www.facebook.com/neva.altaj

TikTok: www.tiktok.com/@author_neva_altaj

Instagram: www.instagram.com/neva_altaj

Amazon Author Page: www.amazon.com/Neva-Altaj

Goodreads: www.goodreads.com/Neva_Altaj

Made in United States
North Haven, CT
21 September 2024